Annetti

by Katie Foth

This is a work of fiction. Names, characters, places, and incidents are either the product of the author's imagination or are used fictitiously. Any resemblance to actual events, places, organizations, or persons, whether living or dead, is entirely coincidental.

Please contact the author on the form on her website at www.katiefoth.com if you experience any formatting or readability issues with this book.

Dedication

To my grandfather Gil, who enriched my childhood and young married life with stories of his mother, and

To my husband Andy, who has enriched my life with his constant love.

Contents

1: Mamma and the Berry Pies

Sorrow seemed an insult to the day I met him. Despite the sunshine streaming through the shop window, I had spent the morning sullenly staring at the empty chair before Mamma's treadle sewing machine.

Papa sat before his machine looking forlorn but determined. He scolded me for my lack of activity. I can still hear him now, with his strong, lilting Norwegian accent: "Annetti, you have done nothing but mope the whole morning. Can you not find something to do? Vurk, child, vurk—that is what you need. Is everything clean?"

"Yes, Papa, of course. Do you see any dirt?"

I watched the corners of his mouth twitch into a half grin as he scrutinized the shop. Bolts of fabric sat neatly on the shelves along the wall to his right. Before him on the counter, a pencil and ledger book awaited more orders. Nine days had passed since I had written in it last. The front window sparkled. The suit and shirt, neatly brushed and pressed, hung in the shop window. Even the lace curtains framing the window hung in precisely even folds.

"Ah!" A gleam brightened his eye, and I smirked as he bent over the dark blue serge in his lap and wiped his finger on the rung of his chair. He inspected the results and puckered his lips in a pout. "You clean as well as your mamma cleaned. I wonder—hmmm. I wonder if you can make a berry pie so good as your mamma too. Ha! A bet! That is what we will make."

"We haven't any berries, Papa."

"Well, we have a basket and two hands that were made to vurk." His light blue eyes twinkled with mischief. "I would bet a week's worth of dirty dishes that you can't make pies like your mamma."

"Will you be making a week's worth of dirty dishes or washing them?" I countered sourly.

I can't help smiling now when I think of that moment. Papa and his "vurk"! But I wasn't smiling then as I picked up the wide, shallow basket heaped with spools of dark thread.

My back was toward Papa. He couldn't have seen the fretful pucker of my lips as I emptied the basket, but he must have heard the sigh that escaped.

"Annetti, Annetti! I wish that I could make you forget. We must—"

"I don't want to forget, Papa."

"*Ja*, I mean the sadness. Why can't you vurk and be happy?"

"I don't know, Papa. The world doesn't seem right."

"*Nei*." Papa sighed. Raw emotion slipped from his voice and settled in an awkward silence between us.

I watched his fingers punch the needle in and out to edge a buttonhole, wishing that my words had not—like a needle—punctured his life with pain. Though barely thirty-five years old, my father looked twice his age when he hunched over his work. He'd lost weight in the last month. He had always been trim, but now his loose clothes made him appear shrunken.

A lone tear trickled down Papa's cheek, and I whispered Mamma's words: "Life has enough pain without making more." Mamma had often said that to me when I'd skinned my knee or burned my finger as a child.

"I want some roses on those cheeks when you come back," Papa ordered, not looking up. Still I waited. "Do not worry about me, Annetti! I have my vurk!"

"Yes, Papa," I murmured, but I knew that those buttonholes wouldn't take all afternoon to finish. He would brush off the lint and press the suit. Perhaps the customer would come for the final fitting, and Papa would be paid by the time I returned.

*   *   *

That July day was as pretty a day as Ashland, Wisconsin, had ever seen. The sun shone warmly on my face, but a cool breeze blew off the lake. I gazed across the blue-gray stretch of Lake Superior.

Why, under God's heaven, can't I be happy on such a gorgeous day?

With a resolute sigh, I started up the dirt road wending through the birches and tall pines.

But then my eyes fell upon a patch of purple mint blossoms among the lush green of the ditch.

Your favorite, Mamma—cones of royal purple blossoms. I had to stop and fill my basket for you. Can you see me here,

Mamma? I wish you could answer me. If only I knew you were happy—if only I could see you again—

But the only answer I found was in the dampness of the gray stone as I ran my finger in the grooves etched there: "Karin Sorenson. Born June 2, 1854; Died May 23, 1888."

Hardly more than a month ago, you were well, Mamma, and I was happy. It isn't fair that you died so young... Life is not right. No—no, death is not right. Oh, is anything right? You, Mamma—I know you didn't want to leave me!

My head ached with such thoughts as I finished arranging the fragrant mint at the base of my mother's gravestone.

How can I forget someone I've lived with, looked to, and loved for every day of fifteen years?

"*Ja*, I mean the sadness," Papa had said.

Mamma's memory seemed so intertwined with the sadness of her loss that I couldn't imagine the sadness ever subsiding. Only the thought of Papa's pain at seeing me so distressed moved me to action. I wasn't doing justice to Papa's "vurk."

There certainly won't be any berry pie, much less roses on my cheeks if I stand here all afternoon, I scolded myself.

I stooped to pick up my equipment. As Papa directed, I had taken the shallow basket with its stained blue gingham lining. But I had also taken the large water pail—just to spite him and prove that I could pick berries with a vengeance. I had packed a lunch in a third basket, the square one with its embroidered lid, the one that Mamma had made when I started school.

I stepped slowly through the tall grass between the wagon ruts, watching the grasshoppers pop up and light on the swaying spears. School! I'd finished grammar school over a year ago. That seemed ages ago. I didn't know any girls who had gone on to high school. For the last year and a half, I'd worked at home, learning seamstress skills from Mamma.

"Annetti!"

Startled, I turned to find my cousin Kirsten racing up the wagon ruts, her petticoats fluttering. Behind her, quite a way back, followed Kelda with the practiced step of one accustomed to wearing fine clothes.

"*Mor* sent us berry-picking," Kirsten panted. Her face glowed with carefree joy, and her long, thin braids bobbed as she spoke. "We're having company for dinner tomorrow. Pastor Lyndahl, and *Mor* said you and Onkel Andrew should come too."

"Papa will be sure to come if Tante Janna serves her famous meatballs," I answered, but inwardly, I cringed. *Not another dinner with the pastor of platitudes!* Papa had upbraided me more than once for my stiff unfriendliness toward the man. I struggled to look civil, not wishing to hurt the feelings of my ten-year-old cousin.

Kirsten blushed and smiled at the compliment to her mother's cooking.

If only roses on my cheeks were that easy, I silently wished.

"You're going berry-picking, aren't you?" Kirsten rattled on, her braids still bobbing. "We're supposed to pick blackberries, *Mor* said, but I'd rather eat raspberries. Wouldn't you, Kelda?"

Kelda had finally caught up with us, and an imperious "Mmmm" was her only reply. At seventeen, she carried herself like a *prima donna* from the operas Tante Janna always raved about watching back in Oslo, near Hønefoss where I'd been born.

I had always felt inadequate in Kelda's presence. She possessed Tante Janna's rare beauty and Onkel Peter's blond curls. Her looks commanded attention, and she knew it full well.

"I want to go with you, Annetti, because you always get the most berries," Kirsten quipped. This time her braids fairly flew through the air as she turned to look at her sister.

Kelda sniffed. "That's because Annetti wades right into the prickles without a thought of scratches." Kelda tossed her head back with an air of importance. She wore a straw hat with a large brim. She'd swept her curls into a loose bun held in place with a hairnet, yet several strands had escaped and framed her face.

Leave it to Kelda to look like a porcelain doll even when she is berry picking. How can she wear a hat on a warm day like this? I'm glad Papa didn't care that I went out bare-headed. I wish this old black muslin dress wasn't so hot, but at least I won't have to worry about tears or stains with this old thing.

"Stop swinging your pail, Kirsten," Kelda ordered. "You'll lose the napkin *Mor* gave you to keep the berries out of the sun."

Oh, my! Her royal highness has issued a command. Poor Kirsten! Must be tough having a bossy older sister like Kelda!

I smiled sideways at Kirsten as she wrinkled her nose, taking the reprimand in silence.

I wonder if Tante Janna was that way with Mamma when they were young. I'm glad Mamma wasn't that way with me—full of prissy criticism.

I switched my equipment to one hand and caught Kirsten's hand with my other. Just like Mamma used to do when Tante Janna used that tone on me, I cast Kristen a sly wink and smiled.

Kristen grinned up at me happily.

Just as I used to do! Mamma always made me feel better.

We walked along in silence until Kirsten screamed, "Raspberries!" and raced off the road.

Kelda sighed. I ignored her and raced after Kirsten. I found a huge clump of blackberry bushes nearby. Kelda followed gingerly. She stood an arm's length from the thorny shoots at the edge of the patch, picking berries and delicately placing them in her basket.

I glanced toward Kristen. She was popping raspberries into her mouth as fast as she could pick them.

Then I dove into the thicket and squatted down, for the shoots most laden with plump, dark berries often can't be seen until one looks up from underneath. I chose the densest spots and picked handfuls, leaving only unripened berries and those half-pecked by birds. The prickles caught my skirt and sleeves and pulled each time I turned to tackle a new spot, but I untangled myself and continued.

The morning passed that way—the red stain growing on Kirsten's lips, the berries *slowly* filling Kelda's basket, and my scratches increasing with each clump I tackled. After we had exhausted a patch, Kirsten would skip merrily on ahead, while Kelda lingered behind with her dainty step. Eventually, I filled both my basket and bucket and started on Kirsten's neglected pail.

The sun stood high overhead when Kelda primly announced that she was finished. I heard Kirsten beg her for a drink of lemonade from the jar in their lunch basket. I couldn't see them, for I had buried myself in another clump of bushes.

I heard a rustling in the leaves near my foot and looked down. A large box turtle stretched its neck toward a low-hanging branch laden with berries.

"Kirsten! I found something you'd like!" I yelled, but there was no reply. I listened carefully. In the distance, I heard the Kirsten's high, girlish chatter along with Kelda's soft, low voice— and someone else's—a man's.

We must be near the road, the one to Washburn. They must have heard someone. Or maybe they saw him.

Hot, sweaty, and scratched, I felt grumpy that they'd left me. But wouldn't Kristen love the box turtle? The thought of showing it off tickled me. I carried Kirsten's basket in one hand and the box turtle in the other until I reached the edge of the thicket where my baskets and bucket sat.

Voices fluttered with the breeze from somewhere beyond. I didn't think further of them, being too distant to distinguish their meaning. I left the berries and scooped up my lunch, thinking that by this time, I deserved a break.

What a sight I must have looked, emerging from the side of that clump in the old black muslin! I hadn't bothered to smoothe the wisps of hair snagged by the prickles. A burst of laughter greeted me, a man's deep, musical laughter.

I spotted Kirsten. Her face was smeared with berry juice and curled in a silly grin. Her blond braids bobbed as she giggled.

My eyes moved to Kelda, pretty as a picture in her blue gingham dress. Her blond curls framed a coy smile. She stood next to a golden-haired man. He leaned against his wooden handcart and shook with laughter.

I moved forward, not totally comprehending what was happening. The man's laughter subsided to a chuckle, and he spoke in Norwegian: "I have come all the way from Norway to see that! All the way to America to find two dumb Norwegians, just like they talk about!"

Kelda glanced from me to Kirsten and tittered politely, but I felt fury rising within me.

How dare he call me dumb?

I was dressed in this awful black muslin, carrying a box turtle, but my face was not smeared with raspberry juice! How dare he compare me to a mere child?

My eyes flashed with wrath. I meant to stare down this rude stranger, but his light blue eyes locked with mine. Those eyes! They dazzled me. Crinkles danced at the corners—just like Papa's. The thought of Papa was somehow calming.

"We dumb Norwegians have to work," I retorted in a crisp Norwegian. I felt my body stiffen with pride. My anger prompted me to switch to English, the one skill I'd mastered better than anyone in

Tante Janna's family: I spoke without an accent. "And I wager that your English is as poor as Papa's."

"*Ja*, you have right," he replied quietly. He scrutinized me. "But I t'ink this 'Papa' is someone I like to meet." The silence that followed seemed enormous. I couldn't think of anything to say. I realized I was staring and dropped my gaze.

Kelda rescued me. "We were just going to have lunch," she informed him. "Would you like to join us?"

"Food is some t'ing I not dislike," the young man replied in his broken English. He grinned. "I eat happy."

I dared a glance up and found him staring impishly at me. His boldness infuriated me. I felt an irritated flush creeping up my neck and cheeks. No doubt I had all the roses Papa could wish for, but I had never expected to procure them by blushing. I would have turned and left right then if Kelda had not interrupted me.

"Annetti, you missed the introductions. This is Lars Sorenson. He just arrived from Norway, and he's on his way to his brother Olin's farm. You remember Olin and Inga from church?" She turned to Lars now. "Annetti is my cousin."

I bristled at the idea of sharing the same last name with this fellow, despite the fact that Sorensons were a dime a dozen in the environs of Ashland. I was acquainted with Olin and Inga, but they were no relation. My eyes fastened coldly on the golden-haired stranger. I supposed that I had to be courteous to some degree.

Kelda is the epitome of manners. If only I could be more like her—even-tempered and gracious!

Yes, I could see that Lars looked a good deal like Olin—lean but muscular, the same broad shoulders and square jaw, the same wavy golden hair and light blue eyes. I gave Kelda a curt nod, but angry thoughts filled my mind.

A shame! It's a downright shame to mix such good looks with such cruel audacity. He laughed at me. He called me dumb!

That awkward silence reigned again. The man's gaze fell to my lunch box. His eyes held a longing look. He pursed his lips and glanced away. He must be truly hungry. Suddenly I felt sorry.

I turned to Kirsten. "I found a box turtle for you, Kirsten." I set both the turtle and the lunch basket down before her. "I'll meet you at home. You know how Tante Janna is about handling fresh berries. I'll take them back before the sun ruins them."

Kelda shrugged and handed me her basket. I nodded a good-bye and walked off, scooping up Kirsten's pail as well as my bucket and basket before I headed down the road.

Balancing four overflowing containers all the way home made my arms ache. By the time I reached Tante Janna's house, my head ached from replaying the encounter.

Why couldn't I have laughed and spoken pleasantly to the man, as Kelda did? For goodness' sake, Annetti! Develop a sense of humor and a modicum of manners! And while we're on the subject of developing skills, how about trying to look like a lady rather than a ten-year-old tomboy who collects turtles? Probably the man will never speak to you again! Oh, fine! What do I care?

Meeting Lars both bothered and scared me. I arrived at Tante Janna's feeling terribly inadequate but determined to grow up. Why not start with those pies? I volunteered to make them for Tante Janna's Sunday dinner. She was delighted with the offer, for she had plenty to finish cleaning before company arrived.

I enjoyed my lease on her large kitchen, and I grew so ambitious that I even made a double baking of my oatmeal rolls in addition to six large blackberry pies. After all, I did have that bet with Papa about the berry pie, and a little success before dessert might help set the outcome for the bet in my favor.

Well, anyway, the oatmeal rolls can't hurt. I've never had anything but raving reviews over how light and delicious they are, and right now I need all the compliments I can curry.

Just when I felt settled and satisfied with my work, Kirsten arrived, chatting a mile a minute, her braids bobbing as she spoke: "That man was real nice, Annetti."

"Really nice, Kirsten."

"Do you think so too?" she asked eagerly.

"No," I replied sternly. "I was merely correcting your grammar."

"He said he hoped you weren't mad. Are you mad, Annetti?"

"When I'm mad, I turn into a purple troll that eats ten-year-old girls. Do I look like a troll?"

Kirsten giggled. "He said he was a dumb Norwegian himself, and after all, he's going to marry a dumb Norwegian," she repeated with a flourish. "Do you think he'll marry me?"

"Certainly not," I declared, wiping my hands on a towel, "because you're going to be eaten by a purple troll."

I roared and chased her out of the kitchen. She screamed and flew out the back screen door, her blond braids flying behind her. I eventually caught her and tumbled onto the grass laughing. I was glad to be wearing the black muslin then.

We stood and brushed ourselves off, still giggling, and I realized I'd laughed for the first time since Mamma died. I'd played the game she had often played with me as a child. And I felt good about that memory—not sad.

I returned to the kitchen to face Kelda's mysterious smile. *Is she mocking my stupidity or dreaming of the stranger?*

I said nothing as I returned to work. The berry-picking incident replayed in my mind's eye as I washed up the dishes I had dirtied in baking. *Lars!*

His name rolled off my lips. I could almost hear the man's laughter ringing in my ears. Insolent laughter. Or maybe I was mistaken? Surely Kirsten's last remark had been a joke—an insolent one. I didn't like jokes about dumb Norwegians. Yet I couldn't help admiring Kelda's attractive ease.

2: Mamma's Mint and Sweet Alyssum

"Are you ready, Annetti?" Papa called upstairs.

"Almost, Papa," I called back.

Papa had finished the suit and received handsome pay for his work. He'd been in a jolly mood when I had arrived home from Tante Janna's, sunburned and flushed from the heat of her big oven.

"Look at your face!" Papa had laughed. "I wanted roses on those cheeks, and I get them everywhere!" He had squeezed my shoulders and pecked both of my cheeks.

The reflection staring at me from the mirror now still looked flushed. I had painstakingly done up my hair in Norwegian braids: One continuous braid circled my head like a golden-brown crown. Now I was struggling to curl the wisps of hair around the edges of my face. Their stubborn straightness frustrated me, and I sighed.

My dress was as fine as any Kelda had ever worn. Mamma had helped me make it last Easter. Was it only four months ago that I had chosen the fabric? The sheer, almost see-through cotton fell in full, freshly starched flounces over my petticoat. I hadn't worn this dress much on account of Mamma's death. I had adored its small lavender flowers and sprigs of forest green against pristine white. I had been so pleased when Mamma had pronounced that I'd done an excellent job of cutting and sewing and pressing and fitting.

The sad memories crept softly into my thoughts, but this morning I brushed them away. *I'm not going to let my feelings rule me today,* I told myself sternly. Patiently, I retied the lavender ribbon on my straw hat. Of course, it wasn't likely that the stranger would be in church this morning after his long trip, but maybe he'd come with Olin's family—not that I planned to waste my time looking for his insolent blue eyes. Still, I'd enjoy flaunting my new look and displaying my indifference to his curious gaze.

"Almost is t'ree minutes long so far," Papa called out teasingly.

With a sigh, I picked up Mamma's Norwegian Bible and swept down the stairs with a hand catching up the full skirt.

"*Uff da!*" Papa exclaimed as I passed him. "You look fine. It is a good t'ing that I had the hair cut yesterday. I would be ashamed to walk with you otherwise."

I pursed my lips, rolled my eyes, and tried to keep a straight face, but I was pleased with Papa's compliment. I didn't mind that he saw me blush.

We lived in the three rooms above the shop. The stairway I descended emptied onto the back stoop, which connected with a little hall to the shop. I hated passing through that hall because there was no way I could avoid looking at the door to the back room. I had hated that room ever since Mamma had died, and I was meticulous about keeping the door shut. There in the back room, Mamma had scraped her elbow on a nail. There her coffin had stood, surrounded by the sickeningly sweet smell of lilacs. This morning the door was open, and the memories made me shudder, but I fought past them.

Between the house and the alley, we kept a garden. I stopped there to pluck one of Mamma's mint blossoms and tuck it into the ribbon of my hat. Then we strode off to the little white wooden building that housed our Norwegian Lutheran church.

I had never cared much for Pastor Lyndahl's sermons. Monotonous and boring couldn't begin to describe them. Even thinking of his exhortations made me tired. But Mamma and Papa had always attended. Nearly everyone I knew did. Maybe they endured the weekly lectures out of duty. Perhaps they came for the pleasure of visiting friends and neighbors afterward. That pleasure was almost worth the imposition, I conceded. But still!

I glanced across the wooden pews as Papa and I moved toward our usual spot three pews from the front. Thorin Hanson sat near the back with his wife Svea and their baby. I had helped Mamma sew Svea's wedding trousseau nearly two years before. My school friends had dubbed the tall, muscular man "Thorin Handsome." A smile started to curl the corners of my mouth, but I pushed the memory from my mind.

We passed Erna and Olaf Fosdick and their neat line of towheads, all in starched white shirts and knickers. Gus Larson sat in the next pew with his two daughters. Widow Thompson and Jenny Lundstrom sat at opposite ends of the pew ahead.

I looked across and spotted Olin Sorenson sitting between his mother and his very pregnant wife. The stranger was not with them. I felt a twinge of disappointment as well as relief.

I had looked back to the sanctuary door at the sound of Kelda's voice, but I didn't catch a glimpse of her dress, for Papa nudged me and winked as he stopped at our pew and paused for me to enter first. He nodded toward the Jenson brothers, whose blue serge suits looked new and quite familiar.

I smiled in acknowledgment and murmured, 'Fine work!"

Papa nodded toward the pew in front of the brothers and looked at me expectantly. There sat the Nyquists with their lovely twin daughters.

"I t'ink soon you start sewing for a double wedding," he whispered loudly as he sat down beside me. "You should put a sign up in the window along wit' a sample of your vurk."

I hardly knew how to respond to his suggestion. My heart jumped at the possibility that he would consider my sewing skills good enough to market, but at the same time I hesitated to boost my hopes for such good fortune.

I studied the Jensons and the Nyquists for a few minutes before shaking my head and whispering, "Papa, Ingrid and Astrida aren't paying the least bit of attention to the Jenson brothers."

"No?" Papa raised his brows in a quizzical arch and twisted his mouth to one side. "Do you not see? They peek behind them every so often and straighten their skirts and whisper to each other."

"Papa!" I whispered, exasperated. "I just turned to peek at Kelda's dress, and I'm straightening my skirts and whispering to you. I suppose that means I'm next in line, does it?"

Papa laughed his deep, full laugh, and then checked it with a cough when both the Nyquists and the Jensons turned to look at him. He dutifully glanced up at the pulpit. My eyes followed Papa's, and I caught my breath in surprise.

The stranger stood there quietly smiling, waiting for the congregation to still. Had he noticed Papa and me? I felt so embarrassed. A hush settled on the small crowd almost immediately.

"Pastor Lyndahl is ill with a fever," he announced in Norwegian. "Being fresh from seminary, I have been asked to fill in and am glad to do so. Please open your hymnbooks and turn to the opening hymn." His eyes roved the congregation as he spoke. I couldn't believe his friendly manner. He almost smiled. Pastor Lyndahl never did that. He always seemed stern.

The stranger's singing wasn't much like Pastor Lyndahl's either. His strong voice and vigorous tone infused life into the liturgy. *What would Pastor Lyndahl think? Wouldn't he call it sacrilegious not to sing with a tone of bland, dutiful reverence? Oh, I'd love to see his face now!*

I glanced up from my hymnal just then. The stranger's eyes caught my curl of a smile. *Lars. Lars Sorenson.* I blushed.

Then I fumed. I had planned to look indifferent. Quickly I lowered my eyes and fastened them on the hymnbook. I focused on Mamma's Bible while he read the Old Testament text. I didn't usually follow along, but finding Deuteronomy chapter six kept my eyes off the stranger. *More commandments,* I muttered to myself.

But the stranger didn't read as Pastor Lyndahl did. I sat entranced by his heartfelt urgency: "Thou shalt love the Lord thy God with all thy heart, with all thy soul, and with all thy might..."

I knew he believed those words, the way he read them. They sounded new to me. *How could they—after fifteen years of church every Sunday? Was I that ignorant?*

We sang another hymn. My eyes stayed glued to the hymnbook entirely this time. Then he read the New Testament text. I had to force my eyes to follow the words, for he read the story just as if he were telling us of yesterday's adventure.

I glanced around as he finished. Every eye was fastened on this golden-haired young man, even those of the little children who usually slept or wiggled unceasingly. An expectant hush filled the sanctuary as he closed his Bible.

I ventured a glance up. Lars Sorenson began telling us about a rich young ruler, just as if the ruler were his admired and beloved friend. This ruler was everything good: well dressed, eager-to-please, sincere, full of respect. The ruler's question showed that he was focused on the right issues: "How would he obtain eternal life?"

The question stung me. Hadn't I almost asked the same question at Mamma's grave? And I wasn't only worried for myself; I was scared for Mamma. *Had she known how to live forever?*

I wanted desperately to know the answer to that question. I listened carefully, wishing the stranger would hurry and tell me, but he took his time instead explaining how a person couldn't arrive at heaven. Keeping the commandments wasn't possible.

Pastor Lyndahl wouldn't like this sermon, I dared to think. I was full of his preaching on living a righteous life and keeping eternity in mind. In some ways, this new thought was uncomfortable. Though Pastor Lyndahl's sermons had always bored me, they were all I had known. And if he were wrong, well—there was no comfort in realizing I'd been mistaken for all of fifteen years, especially when my mother was dead and I was pretty sure that she had not known anything different either. The tears welled up in the corners of my eyes at the thought.

Whatever else the stranger said, I missed. A jumble of questions and arguments filled my mind and pricked my heart. I wanted quiet. I wanted to be alone, to think. The organ and the hum of voices reminded me that I was not.

I followed Papa silently down the aisle to the doors where Lars Sorenson stood shaking hands with those who passed. I didn't want to shake his hand. I didn't want to look at him now, with my head and heart full of worries and struggles.

But there was no other way out. Tears sprang to my eyes, and I brushed them away. I remembered Mamma telling me, "Crying only makes things hurt more, Annetti. Life has enough pain without making things hurt even more."

Shuffling down the aisle with Papa, I battled my feelings and steeled my emotions. "We'll have no more of yesterday," I sternly warned myself.

His handshake was warm and firm, full of a vigor that brought my lowered gaze to meet his. *Those eyes like Papa's, that thick, wavy golden hair...*

"Good morning, Annetti," he greeted me in Norwegian. "Excuse me; I have brought something for you."

I felt Papa's questioning eyes on me, but I said nothing as the stranger handed me the embroidered basket I had left for him yesterday, filled with lunch.

"Thank you for the meal. It was the best I have eaten in months," he continued in Norwegian. He smiled.

I blushed. My lunch had been despicable—cold boiled potatoes with bits of sausage and a spiced oil dressing—leftovers I'd never dream of serving to company. *How am I ever going to explain this to Papa?*

"And you must be Mr. Sorenson?" he continued when I didn't answer. "Good name!"

Papa grinned. For some strange reason, he chose to respond in English: "In this part of the country, Sorensons is—-what you say, Annetti? A dollar a dozen?"

I colored at his inflated rendering of "dime a dozen" but remained silent.

"After what your daughter said, I knew you would be someone good to meet."

His words sounded rehearsed, but the improvement shocked me. *So he cared about what I said!*

Papa glanced at my arched brow, curious, and then asked, "And what would that be? What did Annetti say?"

My eyes flashed at the stranger. *Don't you dare say a word!* I glared at him, but his blue eyes twinkled,

He leaned forward and lowered his voice. "She said that my English is…"

I raised my chin and whipped around, my petticoats swishing as I flew down the steps, full of fury and embarrassment. Papa's deep, full laugh rang out after me.

Kelda caught my arm as I rushed down the walkway past the visiting folk in the churchyard. "Where are you going, Annetti? I thought you were coming to dinner with us."

I looked at her, dumbfounded. I'd been consumed by my feelings again and forgotten. Silently, I wished that she hadn't reminded me. I just wanted to be alone, to be away from that merciless Lars Sorenson, to sit by myself and think.

"*Mor* just asked the new preacher to come—Lars Sorenson. Isn't he interesting?" Kelda's light blue eyes sparkled with boundless excitement.

They're a pair, I realized, my heart feeling wrenched despite my fury. *Light blue eyes and blond curls. Light blue eyes and golden waves. Her beauty, his good looks… What made you think that you could compete, Annetti?*

"She's sending Pastor Lyndahl's family a basket full of dinner." She looked puzzled when I didn't respond. Her look was impatient. "What's wrong with you, Annetti?"

Why did she have to phrase her question that way? I couldn't say anything. The wave of fury turned to jealous rage. I bit my tongue. *I'm wicked, that's what I am. I'm mean and selfish and just plain wicked to feel this way. How will I ever get to heaven?*

She stared at me while I fumbled for an excuse. "I—I don't feel good. I'm going home." I turned and started weakly home, my mind arguing with itself over this half-truth.

The graveyard lay next to the church on the same road as our shop. I dashed through the rows of tall stones until I came to Mamma's grave.

Mamma—oh, Mamma! It does no good to pretend. I don't know the answer. Everything goes wrong. What shall I do?

I wept and sobbed out my cares. After a few minutes, a calm earnestness replaced my tears.

Mamma, did you know how to obtain eternal life? Did you?

My tears fell on the mint blossoms I had placed there yesterday morning. I tore off a small sprig, now flimsy and wilted, intending to press it this afternoon. *To remember you by,* I whispered to Mamma. I opened the embroidered lid of my lunch basket to place it safely inside, but what was this? A small bouquet of sweet alyssum tied with a slender white ribbon! Gently, I picked it up and held it in my hands. I sat there for a long time, looking off across the graveyard and open fields.

"A small gift—to match your lavender eyes," spoke a voice behind me.

I turned, startled. Lars Sorenson stood between two stones in the row behind me. I dropped my gaze and turned my back to him. "My eyes aren't really lavender," I mumbled. "They're only gray, tinged with pale blue."

He didn't leave. He just stood there quietly until I was finally embarrassed enough by his presence to turn and look at him again. Still he didn't speak.

"What do you want?" I asked, forcing myself to look directly at him.

"To say I'm sorry, Annetti. I did not mean to hurt your feelings or make fun of you."

I looked at the ground between us. The grass was so thick and green that blades fell this way and that, nearly asking to be combed into order. I stroked them with my free hand but looked up suddenly as he took a step toward me and then squatted, his face level with mine.

"Your papa told me about your mamma, Annetti," he said softly. "I am sorry—I—you must have loved her dearly."

I looked at the small bouquet in my hand for a long moment and then sighed. "Yes."

I paused and finally looked at him again. "It's all right," I lied. I stood and turned back toward Mamma's gravestone, looking across the field of stones and sorrow. Another long moment passed before the stranger spoke.

"Annetti?"

I turned suddenly at the touch of his hand on my shoulder. There was no way to avoid his direct gaze now, but I no longer felt afraid of it. His blue eyes held mine as he spoke. Somehow I knew there was a shared comfort between us. I had not thought of the loss of others before. Now I remembered. I had seen Olin's mother at church, but never his father—never Lars' father.

To be without Papa? The thought was unbearable. *He must know some of what I feel.*

"Annetti." Lars drew me from my thoughts. "Please come to dinner with us."

I couldn't resist the kind, friendly look his eyes held. Silently I nodded.

3: Kelda and Lars

"Pass the meatballs, please. And the rolls too."

"You can send them this way when you are done, Lars--that is, if there are any left," Papa teased.

Lars grinned as he helped himself to a generous third serving.

"No one makes meatballs so good as you, Janna," Papa stated.

"I will leave you the last two meatballs," Lars replied. "But no one is going to stop me from finishing off these rolls. They are wonderful, Mrs. Nelson."

"That will suit me fine," Papa told him. "The rolls Annetti can make, but the meatballs? I eat those only when my sister-in-law takes pity on me."

Tante Janna threw back her head and laughed her delightful, tinkling laugh, a social feat that Kelda had learned but which I had never mastered. "You poor soul," she teased Papa, fingering the hairpins that held the thick twist of sandy hair atop her head. Everything about Tante Janna was both plump and pleasing, even her hair. Perhaps pleasing was not a strong enough word, for I'd heard even young men call her a *looker*, a woman whose beautiful features captivated the eye.

She fanned her neck before looking at Lars. "I would like to say that I made those rolls too, but Annetti made them yesterday afternoon after she finished the pies." She turned to Papa. "She is a good vurker, Andrew, *ja*?"

Papa smiled and glanced at me sideways. "She has a bet on those pies," Papa warned. "She would not be trying to tip the scales in her favor, now, would she? A whole week of dirty dishes I wash if she wins."

Papa looked at me, his eyebrows arched in mock accusation. I looked back innocently, my mouth puckered and my eyebrows arched, and said not a word. From the corner of my eye, I caught Lars' wide grin. I looked demurely back at the food on my plate.

"I would like to taste those pies," Lars replied. He looked down at his plate. The waves of his thick, golden hair shimmered before me.

Papa just laughed. Then Lars laughed too. A feeling of elation filled me. In that generous moment, I decided it didn't matter that Kelda had spent her time amusing Lars before dinner while I had busied myself helping Tante Janna in the kitchen. It didn't matter that up until now Onkel Peter's stories and Kelda's chatter had held his undivided attention.

"I tell you one thing," he continued. "Good meal is hard for a poor seminary student to find. Sometime I think I fast in the wilderness—forty days and forty nights."

"Doesn't seem to have hurt you much," Onkel Peter joked. His silver-white curls jiggled as he chuckled. He spoke with only a touch of accent, perhaps because of the constant contact he had with neighboring folk who depended on his skills as a doctor.

"But you must have learned a great deal," Onkel Peter continued. "I have a patient who asked me nearly the same question as your sermon. He's a good man. He takes care of his family, goes to church regularly, helps his neighbors. You couldn't ask for a finer person. His question distressed me, but then, those who face death? Well, they think of these things."

A shiver ran up my spine at these words. Onkel Peter paused and looked at Tante Janna gravely. "It is another case of blood poisoning, Janna."

A hush fell across the table. I looked down at my hands, folded in my lap, fighting the wave of sadness those words brought. Mamma had died of blood poisoning. *But I am not the only person who has had to deal with death,* I told myself firmly. *There's Papa. Mamma was his wife. And Tante Janna. Mamma was her sister. And Lars. His father had died too.* I looked up and found Lars gazing at me as he spoke.

"*Ja,* but it is good he is asking." He turned to Onkel Peter. "He may be halfway to heaven. He knows he has a need. He realizes he cannot get there by himself."

Everyone sat, silent and thoughtful. I sat wondering if I was halfway to heaven. *Hadn't I asked myself the same question this very morning?*

"I would be glad to visit that man with you, if you would like," Lars offered. "We could go this afternoon, before I walk home."

"Walk home, no-t'ing!" Tante Janna interjected. The beautiful lines of her plump face flushed with color as she spoke. "Peter can take you. And there is pie before you go visiting."

I watched her eyes take in Kelda's rapturous gaze. A tender smile pulled at Tante Janna's lips. Her glance swept on around the table, past Onkel Peter's approving nod and Kirsten's innocent stare. Her gaze landed on me. "Annetti, would you mind serving dessert?"

"Of course not," I replied with forced brightness. I slipped from my chair and headed toward the kitchen.

"I heard you had quite a surprise on the way to your brother's yesterday," she teased. "Some-t'ing about a bear, Kirsten says?"

Alone in the kitchen, I blushed to myself, embarrassed. *Bear?* I had missed that part. *Had Lars mistaken me—in that horrid black muslin dress—for a bear grousing for berries? So maybe he meant to call himself dumb?* I began slicing through the dark gel and lattice top of the first pie. The pies had turned out beautifully, but that fact no longer seemed important.

I took my time, grateful for the excuse to be alone and to think. Tante Janna had loved Mamma, her younger, plainer, poorer sister. But I had never seen her sad even when Mamma died in her arms—kind, but not sad. She had smiled tenderly and said softly: "Precious in the sight of the Lord is the death of His saints."

Did she know something about Mamma and heaven that I didn't know? What was it that seemed to bring her abounding strength in the face of loss? I thought of all the sorrow and sadness I had faced in the past months. *Does facing sorrow make one strong? How can it, when it hurts so much? Tante Janna is strong, just as Papa is strong.*

I thought of Lars and of the strength of character he seemed to possess. He seemed happy and carefree, and yet he had faced the subject of death with serious attention. Was that due to faith? He was a preacher, so he had to have faith. His faith did not consist of dull repetitions of dry words from a dusty old book. His faith was— exactly what? I needed to find that out.

I slid a triangle of pie onto the last plate, wiped my hands, and carried three of the plates through the door to the dining room. I stood there a moment, taking in the sight. Onkel Peter sat at the left end; Tante Janna presided over the right end. Kirsten and Papa sat with their backs toward me. My chair, between Papa and Tante Janna, had been pushed smartly up to the table—Papa's doing probably.

Across the table sat Kelda and Lars, wrapped in their own conversation. I hadn't heard what Kelda had said, but Lars was smiling at her. "I would like that very much," he was saying. Kelda was smiling sweetly and looking at him with an adoration that made me sick at heart. My eyes bounced from his blue eyes to her blue eyes, his smile to her smile—how it hurt!

Papa was teasing Kirsten, while Onkel Peter abetted him and Tante Janna teasingly admonished them both to stop. I delivered the pieces of pie quietly and unnoticed. As I returned to the kitchen to fetch the remaining three pieces, I heard Lars saying to Onkel Peter, "You have two lovely daughters."

"Actually, we have three," Onkel Peter replied. "Our daughter Katrina is married and lives in Cloquet, Minnesota. She is twenty-two and has a little son, Dieter, and one on the way."

"Cloquet?" Lars asked. "Where is that?"

"You sailed inland through the St. Lawrence Seaway and the Great Lakes, right? Ontario, Eerie, Huron, Superior."

Lars nodded. "I know Ashland on the Superior, *ja.*"

"Good. Duluth is about seventy miles farther west. Its beauty comes close to that of the fiords. Cloquet is about twenty miles southwest of Duluth. It's a lumber town, started up to clear a driftwood jam on the St. Louis River. The first sawmill was built there about ten years ago. Now they float lumber all along the St. Louis River to sawmills in Cloquet."

"A good thing for a carpenter!" Lars exclaimed brightly.

"But a bad thing for a beautiful daughter," Tante Janna countered with a tinge of animosity. "The town is rustic."

"What do you expect?" Onkel Peter demanded. "It only became a village in 1884."

"Ttch! It is mostly a jumble of thin board houses one must share with coarse, uneducated men. Imagine! Katrina lives in a boarding house with only a room for her whole family, and they have a four-year-old boy."

"But it's a large room, Janna. And after all, Nils must keep his business afloat while they're saving to build a house. The town is growing, and their housing situation will change soon enough," Onkel Peter replied firmly. "Nils Gregerson has done well for himself, and we couldn't have asked for a better man to take care of our oldest daughter."

Lars smiled. His blue eyes scanned past Kirsten and Onkel Peter and settled on Kelda as he spoke: "You are blessed of God to have such a good family."

I had whisked silently through the door, delivering the other plates of pie. I returned to the kitchen unnoticed. The words rankled in my mind—words Lars meant for good, but they weren't words about me. I wrapped myself in Tante Janna's large apron and poured some of the water heating on the back of the stove into the dishpan.

Deep in thought, I washed dishes. I would never be as lovely as Kelda is. I was like Mamma, a plain face with straight brown hair. I could pretend not to care that I wasn't a ravishing beauty, but I did care. Kelda was pretty, more than pretty, and the Nelsons were blessed, Lars said, to have such a good family. His words made me feel so alone. I had no lovely sisters. I had no mother. I had no faith.

I had all the pots and pans washed by the time Tante Janna came bustling into the kitchen. "Oh, Annetti, thank you! I told you, Andrew," she said to Papa, who had followed her with a stack of plates and silverware, "she is a good vurker."

"*Ja,*" I said with forced cheer. "We dumb Norwegians have to vurk." Papa laughed. I smiled at him somewhat grimly, and he laughed all the louder.

"What am I missing?" Lars called from the doorway.

I escaped by carrying the dishpan full of dirty water out the back door. I dumped it carefully over the edge, letting just a trickle fall at the base of the trumpet vines that grew up the trellises on either side of the back porch. Then I stood there a moment enjoying the warm breeze and bright sun.

"She says the funniest things," I heard Kelda declare with a giggle. Then the back door slammed, and I heard the voices of Onkel Peter and Lars. I slipped around the side of the porch as they came down the steps. I stood there, swathed in Tante Janna's apron, brushing the wilted bangs from my forehead with my wrist, watching them hitch up the surrey. I didn't think they had noticed me until Lars waved.

Papa was drying pots and pans when I returned, but he didn't stay long, for Tante Janna shooed him out of the kitchen. "Such a man!" she scolded. "This is our vurk, you thief!" Papa just grinned. Mechanically, I refilled the dishpan and started on the cups and glasses.

Kelda came up beside me with a large white dishtowel in her hands. She sighed, picked up a glass, and absentmindedly began to wipe it dry. She dried one glass for every three I washed, but she didn't seem to notice. When Tante Janna left to change the tablecloth, she asked dreamily, "Isn't he handsome, Annetti?"

How like Kelda! Her starry-eyed manner irritated me. I aimed to annoy her with my brusque, business-like tone. "Who?" I asked.

Kelda stared at me a moment and then giggled. "Oh, you would joke! I meant Lars, of course. He has the bluest eyes. Surely you've noticed." She emphasized that last word and gave me one of her coy smiles.

Pretty as a picture, even when she's drying dishes, I thought with envy, but I shrugged in an off-hand manner. "Ashland is full of people with blue eyes."

"Really, Annetti," she scolded with a disgusted huff. "I don't understand you. Perhaps when you're seventeen, like me, you'll..." Her voice trailed off as Tante Janna returned to the kitchen with the soiled tablecloth and napkins, but she cast me a most despairing glance.

4: The Buggy Ride

I walked home alone that afternoon, carrying only my embroidered lunch basket. Papa had left after Tante Janna's refusal to have him underfoot in the kitchen. Despite the fact that there was nothing else to do on a Sunday afternoon, I had no desire to stay and humor Kirsten or to endure Kelda's condescending airs. I wished that I could do something useful, even if it was picking berries for jam, but Papa would never hear of it. *Not on Sunday.*

Ashland was quiet. I ambled slowly past the big houses on the Nelsons' street, admiring the intricate trim. When the street ended at the main road along the shore of Lake Superior, I turned left and walked past the Chequamegon Hotel, a popular summer resort of the wealthy, until I came to our shop. The shop was closed, of course, and I had just started toward the narrow walk leading around the side of the building to the back porch when I heard the steady clop of horses' hooves and the rattle of wheels on the brick road. I turned to see Onkel Peter in his surrey with Lars beside him. I started toward the narrow walk again, but Onkel Peter had seen me.

"Annetti! Come. Join us! A ride out in the fresh air will do you good." Reining the horses to a stop before me, he sat in his black suit and hat, waiting for my reply.

"Do I still need fresh air after all the sunburn I managed to acquire yesterday?" I asked him, hoping to find a way to decline.

Onkel Peter threw back his head and boomed out a long, rolling laugh. Of course, Papa heard him and poked his head out of the upstairs window. My comment had to be repeated and laughed over once more before Papa himself insisted that I did indeed need more fresh air. I scowled back at Papa, but he only laughed again and winked at me.

I sighed and looked at Onkel Peter's surrey. Neither Papa nor Onkel Peter knew how much I dreaded climbing up. The way the horses shook their harness always made me nervous, and I envisioned myself slipping or catching my dress in the wheel. But Lars had jumped down and circled around the back of the surrey while I hesitated. Without asking, he helped me up and tucked the dust blanket around the edges of my skirt. I blushed at all the attention and murmured my thanks, trying to ignore the prickles of excitement I felt inside.

I sat on one side of Onkel Peter. Lars sat on the other. We bumped along in silence, and I wondered if my presence was making conversation awkward. I tried to think of something to say—something less trite than a comment on the weather. They had been out to visit the man with blood poisoning. *I could ask how their call went,* I thought. *But what if the man had—*-I winced. *Perhaps the man's death explained their silence.*

"You look awfully serious, Annetti," Onkel Peter finally said.

"That is a common complaint about my face these days," I replied. "I was wondering about your patient. How is he doing?"

Onkel Peter looked surprised. "The patient is coming along fine. Much better than the last time I saw him, although I do not know that I deserve any credit for the improvement. One thing disturbs me, though." He turned to Lars. "The man listened to what you said, but he did not believe you. I could see it in his eyes."

"*Ja.* Many believe not right away. The vurking of the Holy Spirit in man's heart—that takes time."

"He appears to be blessed with more time."

"*Ja,* that is good," Lars replied. He laughed and shook his golden head of hair. "Now me—I was such a stubborn fellow! It took years."

"Years?" Onkel Peter countered. "From your ancient age of what? Twenty-five, years? That could mean but two or three years of stubborn disbelief."

From the corner of my eye I watched Lars' grin and his dancing light blue eyes. "Oh, *nei!* Over sixteen, it was. Papa was very strict, and I was just as stubborn. Olin—he was a good boy. Did what Papa wanted, believed what Papa wanted. But not I. I did not even want to listen."

I leaned forward slightly and looked at Lars curiously. "What changed your mind?"

"A young man with whom I vurked. '*Ja,* you can do what you want,' he would say. 'If you want to be stupid just because your father is not—what do I care?' He would tease me so. I had to think why I did not want to believe Papa's preaching. I think on the gospel a long time. Papa left for America with Olin and Mamma. I was stubborn and did not want to go. I ran away."

My eyes opened wide in shock of such an idea. "But where did you go?"

"To Sweden, and then to sea as a ship's carpenter, not knowing that the captain who signed me on was a man of God. He only sailed the coasts of Sweden, and his family sailed with him. Every morning and evening, we read the Bible and prayed. I listened only because of Margetta, his daughter. She was beautiful, so beautiful. Sometimes she would watch as I vurked, and we would talk about the nature of God. 'I think I know God already,' I tell her. 'He is stern judge like my father.'

"She laughed. 'I see you have a very narrow viewpoint,' she told me. 'But God is infinite—infinitely wise, infinitely good, much more than you can ever think.' "

"'How do you know these things?' I ask her."

"She laughed again and said she *listens* when the captain reads. So I listen too. The words of the Gospels—they stay in my heart and mind. I try not to believe them, but I know they are true and right, and I finally believe." He paused and stared ahead with a distant hurt in his eyes, a look I knew altogether too well.

"What happened to her?" I asked gently.

He did not answer right away. "She died of pneumonia just before I turned nineteen—a few months after our marriage. I went home to Trondheim. The neighbors gave me Papa's address." A smile played on his lips. "He was overjoyed to hear from me—and to hear that I now believed. I never realized until then how much he loved me—*ja*, and I had never realized how great a love God had for me. I wanted to do everything for Him. I heard of a seminary in Oslo. I went to study, and now I am here."

Tears flowed down my cheeks, and I leaned back against the black leather cushions of the surrey, wishing to hide. "But your father—?"

"It is all right, Annetti. He sees me now. He still loves me from where he is."

I wished with all my heart that I could feel with the same certainty the presence of my mother's love, but I felt nothing—only sorrow. If only I could know this great love of God that Lars knew—yet I felt only loneliness, emptiness, and a great yearning. A deep sadness filled my heart as I thought of Mamma.

Onkel Peter began telling of his years as a young surgeon in the Civil War, but I was too distracted with my thoughts to pay close attention. His words seemed to rumble on with the wheels as we passed the neat fields and young orchards.

Then all of a sudden we were there. We turned into the long drive beside the square white farmhouse and stopped where it looped before the back porch. Lars jumped off. I nodded to him and smiled slightly, my eyes still teary. But instead of shaking the reins and bidding goodbye, Onkel Peter held the horses and continued talking.

I saw the porch door open, and Olin and Inga emerged. They were calling for Onkel Peter to stop and have a dish of tea and hot scones. I felt embarrassed to be there, afraid I might not know what to say if I were expected to visit. Inga was round with child, and I blushed to think I might have to bear conversation on that unknown subject.

I held my breath and hoped that Onkel Peter would excuse himself and hurry home. He did not. He climbed down from the surrey and tied the reins around the hitching post, leaving me to descend with the help of Lars. The feel of his hands on my waist as he lifted me down sent shivers through my body. One glance at his penetrating blue eyes made me lower my gaze and blush. A tear trickled down my cheek.

Self-conscious, I turned slightly away from the group, casting my eyes across the openness of the farm. The barn stood to my right, the tool shed before me, and the house and the knot of people to my left. Behind me—I gazed with pleasure. Across the long green yard stretched a garden, all the way from the barnyard to the road. Shades of lush green rose up from the dark earth in neat rows. I spotted a huge elm reigning over a small white bench in the side yard, and I knew at once where I wished to be.

"Won't you come in?" Inga was asking me.

"I'd love to look at your garden if I could," I asked almost in a whisper.

Inga nodded and a pleased smile spread across her face. "It is Adelle's garden. She would love for you to look."

"Thank you," I murmured. I stood and watched the others head toward the porch, then turned and wandered through the yard to the edge of the garden. I passed rows of bush beans--purple, yellow wax, and green. I passed the spidery green of carrot tops, the sprawling vines of squash, the shoots of onions, walls of pea plants climbing their frames of string, squat broad-leafed pie plants--I had never seen such a magnificent garden. I paused near the mosaic of herbs across from the elm tree. "Parsley, chives, dill," I recited. "Sage, and that must be thyme and basil and—and mint...mint." I could feel the tears welling up in my eyes.

I couldn't look at mint without thinking of Mamma. Somehow it brought the memories of her so close, and yet she was so far away. *Is she in heaven?* I looked up at the brilliant blue sky and wondered how far away heaven was, what it looked like. *Is Mamma happy there? Is she wrapped in the arms of God's love so fully that she could feel the warmth? Could she see me?* I felt so empty. *How would I ever know God's love,* I wondered—*it seemed so hard to believe, so impossible to feel midst my sorrow.*

The tufts of long, soft grass flopped this way and that. I stepped through the tresses and sat on the white bench under the elm, sighing in despair. My mind went back to the morning's sermon, to the rich young ruler and his question of how to obtain eternal life. I thought of the text, "Thou shalt love the Lord thy God with all thy heart, with all thy soul, with all thy mind." *How can I love God if I don't even know Him?*

My eyes fell upon a circlet of sweet alyssum edged with flagstone. I bit my lip and opened my embroidered lunch box. Inside lay a bouquet of the same alyssum, tied with a thin white ribbon. Its kindness had surprised me at Mamma's grave. My feelings tumbled one upon another. I felt wretched and unworthy. I bit my lip to hold the tears back, but I couldn't. I was alone, and I wept.

5: Adelle

I don't know how much time had passed when I finally looked up and out across the garden, an empty sorrow having replaced my tears. I sat motionless until I heard the clap of a screen door and footsteps on a wooden porch. I turned to see the crisply dressed figure of Olin's mother rounding the corner of the house. She was Lars' mother too, I remembered, and I looked down into my lap at the thought.

"Inga told me you were here looking at the— Why, child! You are not happy!" She sat down beside me and slipped her arm around my shoulders. "What is it, dear?"

I hesitated. Looking timidly into her eyes and trembling, I glanced hurriedly back down at my hands, folded in my lap. I did not dare to speak, for I did not know how to choose words that encompassed my despair. I felt the light warmth of her arm still circling my shoulder and the patient kindness of her gaze. I stared out at the garden.

"I don't know," I finally whispered. "I miss Mamma, and I feel so hopeless, so...so—inadequate." I looked down at my hands again and bit my lip, but she didn't interrupt. "I hope Mamma's in heaven. I—I don't think I'll ever get there."

"Annetti--" The soft calm of her voice startled me, and I realized she had taken my hands in hers, grasping them in a firm, almost urgent squeeze. "Annetti, I knew your mamma, and she loved the Lord in her own quiet way. But none of us is good enough for heaven of ourselves. That is the beauty of God's way. He loved us. He loves you, Annetti."

"But I don't love Him," I blurted out, choking down a sob. "I don't even know Him."

"*Ja*, perhaps. And perhaps you have known Him all the time but never realized that He gave His Son to die for *you*, because of the things *you* have done wrong."

I looked up into her eyes, startled. "I've heard those words many times, but I never thought of them like that."

She smiled at me for a long moment before she spoke, while I studied the glint in her azure eyes. "Knowledge and faith—they are not the same thing. Knowledge comes from seeing and hearing, but faith—faith is believing the truth of God's words to us."

I nodded slowly. The realization spread through my being a shaft of hope. "And believing—how do you believe?"

She paused a moment, cocking her head to one side, then spoke with a cautious hesitation between her words. "You decide. You trust that something is true. You put your hope in that truth."

My eyes locked with hers for a long moment. She was silent, but I knew she was inwardly asking me, "Do you?"

I gazed out over the garden, pondering that question. In ways I did not want to believe. I wanted to see and to feel that God loved me, Annetti—and that He loved Mamma. *God,* I called out in my mind, *I don't know You. I wish I did. I can't say I trust, but I want to believe. Oh, God, I want to.*

I watched the sweet peas nod and bob in the gentle breeze, and I waited. No great surge of joy or heartwarming love enveloped me. Yet, in the quiet calmness of my soul, I knew with all of my being that what she said—what I had learned of God in church—was true and right. I turned to her with a slight smile.

"Come, Annetti," she said gently. "We will look at the garden before you go." She stood and led me toward the section of herbs. "You have a garden at home?"

I nodded shyly, following behind her. "We live in town, of course, and we only keep a small back yard of a garden. We have a few herbs and flowers. But this garden—" I stopped and gazed about me. "It stretches row upon row. It's like—like rolls of ribbon all different hues of green, all stretched out over a table of dark velvet."

She smiled at me. "That sounds pretty, when you speak about it in that way. They are all different colors too, now that I think to notice."

"And different heights, with different leaves." I knelt down and fingered the saw-toothed leaves of a low bushy plant. "I don't think I know what plant this is." I looked up at her and blushed. "I don't know what to call you. It sounds funny to say *Mrs. Sorenson*."

"Then you may call me Adelle." She responded. "Those are strawberries—some of the boys' favorite. They make good jam mostly. They bear in June, but maybe I find you a leftover, *ja*?" She bent over and brushed across the row with her hand, parting the leaves. "*Nei.* Well, I give you a few plants, and you can make a bit of jam next year."

"I couldn't let you do that," I objected. "You'll have gaps in your rows then."

"*Nei, nei*—I have to thin them later anyway. How many would you like? You have a little walk to plant them by, maybe?"

I nodded.

"Good. We will get you a little crate to put them in, and you can give them a good watering when you get home."

I followed Adelle across the yard to the shed, noticing how fresh her bright blue poplin dress and white apron looked. She stood about my height but looked stout and much plainer than I looked in my fine Sunday dress. *Yet the plainness becomes her,* I thought. She possessed the glow of a satisfied, mature woman. I vowed to become like her, plain and yet compelling.

Adelle entered the shed and turned abruptly. "You stay here. No sense to chance soiling that Sunday dress," she commanded. So I stood in the doorway and watched her rummage through the wooden crates in the dimness of the shed. She chose a long shallow tray, found a hand shovel, and emerged from the shed, blinking in the bright sun.

She hesitated there a moment, her sandy hair showing glints of silver. She had it done up in braids, wound around her head like mine. She tucked a short strand behind her ear. The blue of her eyes matched the brightness of her dress and the brilliance of the sky. Goodness and kindness seemed to shine from her eyes. *Will I emanate such virtues when I am old? Will I possess that beauty of character? I must try.*

Perhaps she sensed my thoughts, or perhaps she merely marked the admiration in my eyes, for she smiled at me and took my arm as we walked, surveying the garden once more.

"Annetti, your whole life is before you like the earth of this garden, you see? You must plant good seeds, water them, and pull out the weeds of selfishness and sin. Then you have a good garden, a good life, *ja?* You are young. One must take good care of herself, both inside and out."

I nodded and looked out across the huge garden, thinking of all the plowing and planting and mulching and hoeing such a garden would require. "It looks to be a great deal of work," I commented. "I mean—it certainly seems as if it would be a great deal easier to look back across a spring of hard work—or a whole lifetime for that matter—than it would be to look forward."

Adelle had begun digging up a strawberry plant, but at my comment she stopped and looked out across the garden. "*Ja*, but the reward of vurk well done—that makes life worth everything. And we are ever ones to vurk."

I couldn't help laughing. "Not you too!" I thought of Papa and his "vurk," and I blushed to think of my sour comment to Lars that first day, "We dumb Norwegians have to vurk."

She smiled up at me. "*Ja*. When God has blessed us with the ability to give, to vurk—we must use it. *Uff da*! Look at these hands! I think we have enough. You can plant these in the evening when it is cool. Dig a little hole; fill it with water, then put in the plant. They will need a little water every day to get a good start."

Our walk back to the house was silent. Adelle went inside the house to wash. I tucked the tray of strawberry plants under the seat of the surrey and waited, keeping my distance from the horses. I stood with my back to the house, looking out over the garden, thinking about what Adelle had said, when I heard the clap of the screen door again. I turned to see Lars coming toward me, his eyes twinkling.

"Annetti, tell me how you charmed Mamma out of one of her precious jars of strawberry jam," he teased, his blue eyes crinkling at the corners like Papa's. "She sent me to the cellar for it, and it is a good thing she is writing out the recipe so that you can make me a replacement."

"You're as bad as Papa about teasing," I returned with a grin. "You know very well there will be no more strawberries until next June."

"You do not know how much I love Mamma's strawberry jam," he persisted. "I think you should give me a jar of blackberry jam at least."

"That's a clever idea," I stated, enjoying the banter and the attentive gaze of his heavenly blue eyes. Then I thought of Kelda and the memory of his blue eyes fastened with hers. *What a fool I am becoming,* I scolded myself. I said nothing to Lars—simply took the jar of jam from him and tucked it under the seat of the surrey next to the tray of plants.

"You have told me before that I was as bad as your Papa." He paused, and I could see his grin from the corner of my eye as I finished. "But I like your Papa. You like him too, I can tell. Perhaps you like me as much as you like your Papa?"

I blushed, not knowing what to say. His teasing did remind me of Papa.

"I like you," he stated. "I wish you would like me as much."

I turned toward him, startled. The words spilled from my mouth before I could check them. "And I wish you would like me as much as you like certain people with *blue* eyes," I retorted hotly, my eyes flashing with emotion. Then I blushed, embarrassed at having betrayed my true feelings.

He just grinned at me. "Do that again. I love it."

"Do what?" I asked, politely indignant, tossing my head and glaring at his annoying grin.

"That." He threw his head back and laughed.

"I fail to see what is so humorous," I stated tartly.

"Your eyes—they are so—so—"

"Lavender? Thank you, Reverend Sorenson. You are most observant."

He bowed in mock reply. Just then Onkel Peter appeared, with Olin and Inga and Adelle behind him. I blushed to be found standing there with Lars, but no one seemed to notice or think anything of it.

"Come, Annetti. We'd best be off," Onkel Peter was saying. He climbed into the surrey and reached out his hand to help me up.

I glanced toward the horses, hesitant, then caught up the skirt of my dress with one hand and grasped Onkel Peter's with the other.

Adelle moved close to help me tuck in the dust blanket. "I have brought you my recipe for strawberry jam," she announced, handing up a folded piece of paper.

"I have heard tales of your strawberry jam, Mrs. Sorenson," Onkel Peter complimented. "My wife would like that recipe too, but I thought it was a family secret."

"I think it will be safe with Annetti," she replied.

"You should not give it away for no-t'ing," Lars objected teasingly. "Mamma, you could at least get Annetti's recipe for oatmeal rolls or blackberry pie. They are wonderful! The best piece of baking I have tasted in a long time."

She turned and looked at him in stark amazement, her fists perched sternly on her hips. "I beg your pardon! Did you or did you not just consume three of my scones?"

"It was four," Lars quipped with a grin. "I snitched another when you weren't looking."

We all laughed. Lars winked at me, and I blushed, hoping no one else had noticed. A warm, pleasant feeling filled my heart.

Our ride home was a gentle, pleasant trip. Onkel Peter didn't talk much. We just enjoyed the scenery. He must have said something to his family that evening, though, for the next day Kelda paid me a special visit at the shop. She was curious about everything.

Thank goodness Papa was down at the docks picking up a new shipment of fall fabrics when she came! I could never have acted so nonchalant under Papa's scrutinizing eyes, nor would I have heard the end of his teasing. I frustrated Kelda to no end with my indifferent answers. She finally shook her delicate blond curls and sighed in exasperation at my series of "I don't know," "I never noticed," and "Not much."

"Gracious, Annetti!" she complained. "When are you ever going to wake up? I should think you're well on your way to being an old maid. I certainly don't intend to be one!" And off she trounced, her curls shaking in indignation.

I smiled to myself at her scolding. I was awake—awake enough to know better than to tell her what she wanted to hear.

6: Blackberry Jam

I stood at the back of the shop nearly three weeks later fitting the jackets of the Nyquist twins' new fall outfits on Mamma's dressmaking form. The soft blue wool slipped pleasantly between my fingers as I pinned the tucks and button loops in place. I had been quite busy with this order but nonetheless very pleased. This order was strictly mine. Though Papa would stoop to wash a whole week's worth of dirty dishes, he refused to tailor women's clothing. Dressmaking—as he called it—was purely women's business and should be the work of a seamstress.

Mamma had been a seamstress, much to Tante Janna's disdain. I had never quite figured out how she could adore Mamma's creations, yet consider Mamma's business an embarrassment. Mamma never spoke to me of their disagreements, but somehow I came to understand that Tante Janna's large, well-furnished house had something to do with the issue.

Mamma had rarely complained, even when she was dying. Despite Papa's austere, business-like preferences, Mamma had insisted on decorating the waiting room of the tailor shop to look like a parlor. She had demanded this courtesy outright for *her* customers, and when Papa saw her determination, he bent to her will.

Mamma had hung a lacy curtain at the store window and had cajoled Papa into buying a two-tiered fluted mahogany table and two fancy side chairs covered with dark, flowery needlepoint. Later she had purchased a large oval mirror to hang across from the table and had even ordered a Persian rug. Papa had fussed, of course, but she had reminded him that her earnings had more than covered these purchases.

I smile to think of how much she enjoyed those treasures. I think that they meant so much to her because we did not have a parlor in which to entertain as other ladies did, as Tante Janna did. Although she could not live on par with her respectable customers, she had found an excuse for obtaining at least a few of the luxuries they took for granted.

Perhaps that had also been the excuse for our large flower and herb garden. Papa would tease Mamma about growing something edible, but Mamma liked having fresh flowers, whenever possible, in the vase on the little mahogany table. She had liked the fragrance of her homemade potpourri warming on the pot-bellied stove in the winter. She had adored the delicate freshness of tiny sachet bags along the shelves of her fabrics.

Papa grumbled about wasting work time and starving in style, but it was Mamma's subscription to *Godey's Lady's Book* that sparked the only on-going disagreement that I remembered my parents having. *Godey's Lady's Book* was a magazine that Mamma kept on the little mahogany table for ideas as well as for the enjoyment of her customers. Ladies used to stop by our shop to look at the new fashions whenever we received a new issue.

In some ways, that magazine was Mamma's entrance into the social lives of her customers. Papa had fussed over the cost of that luxury, as well as over the commotion the ladies made looking at that book. He fussed so regularly that Mamma finally made a joke of the issue.

After Mamma's death, Papa had not wanted to renew the subscription. I had wanted nothing to change. I loved the things Mamma had treasured. Those details seemed a vital connection to life itself. I had not been able to convince Papa to keep the subscription until I had used her normal words of response to his complaints on the subject: "*Ja*, now. You know as well as I do that you love the latest gossip as much as they do, only you are too embarrassed to show it. Don't think I have not noticed you listening to us talk and looking at that book later when you think I don't see."

So we continued the subscription. The latest issue of the magazine still rested on the little mahogany table, although it had made considerably less commotion since Mamma's death. Perhaps ladies had hesitated to underscore Papa's loss. Nevertheless, I had continued to pour over *Godey's Lady's Book*.

One afternoon, the slender Nyquist twins stopped in the shop to consult it, and when they remarked on the new wool suits promoted in the latest edition, I was ready to discuss the styles. I had dreamed about how I would design a new outfit from each of the wools Papa had brought home in the last shipment. As the twins paged through the pictures, I pointed out my favorite style and suggested it would look wonderful in the new pale blue wool. It had arrived much to Papa's chagrin over failing to have had his standard order changed, an order which had always included fabrics for Mamma's side of the business.

I had offered to make the suits. The twins seemed a bit unsure at first, but I reminded them that I had made the dress I had worn the previous Sunday—that Mamma had taught me. Mamma's expertise was missed, I could tell, and the twins were eager to have it replaced.

"What did I tell you?" Papa teased. "The Jenson brothers took them buggy riding on Sunday afternoon. And now the twins want new Sunday clothes. I think you should start on those wedding dresses."

"Accepting a buggy ride does not constitute an engagement to marry, Papa," I told him tartly, but he just laughed.

"And what do you know about that?" he teased. His grin widened when I blushed, and the corners of his blue eyes crinkled, reminding me of Lars. I had not wanted to tell him the details of my ride with Onkel Peter and Lars, and I wondered what Onkel Peter had told him.

"I know more than you think," I retorted and turned silent. The suggestion embarrassed me. I could imagine Papa teasing me about a friendship with Lars. I had taken the twins' measurements and was calculating the exact yardage. Then, to be sure, I measured the yardage on the bolt and frowned. "It's enough," I told Papa. "But I won't be able to make many mistakes."

"Are you sure you can do it?" he asked. I could read the question marks in his eyes.

"I suppose it is a daring adventure with my lack of experience, but I think I can manage if you'll look over my shoulder now and then and make a few suggestions."

Papa nodded but still looked unsure. I think that he has now changed his mind. I caught him grinning at me several times as I planned and cut and stitched and measured, ripped open seams, sewed them back together again, and pressed everything in place.

After another Sunday's buggy ride with the Jensons, Papa began teasing me with a proud wink and an I-told-you-so nod every time either party passed by the shop. "*Ja*, you can be sure this is only their first order."

"Oh, Papa, you exaggerate," I objected, not letting myself hope for more work yet.

"You don't think the wedding dress comes next? Ah! You are right! I forget. They must order a trousseau first."

"Honestly, Papa, I think you need some work." That response came without thinking. It was something Mamma used to say when Papa teased her too much, although I had not said it with the same inflections with which Mamma pronounced the fact: "I *t'ink* you need some *vurk*."

Papa was quiet at the comment, and I felt bad not only because I had made him miss Mamma but because the fact was true. He did need work. He had not received any orders since the Jenson brothers' suits, and Papa never liked being without his "vurk."

Papa sat on his sewing machine stool, turned toward me, watching me pin the facings in place. I didn't ever remember seeing him discouraged, as he appeared now. He looked tired of life, and it bothered me—scared me almost. He had consistently been strong and cheerful, and I wanted him that way always.

I realized then that Papa had probably felt the same way about me after Mamma died. It had bothered him that I had not been cheerful and strong. Perhaps he was right about the virtues of his "vurk." I had not moped about the house since I landed the twins' order. In fact, I had not even visited Mamma's grave in the last three weeks, though I had thought plenty about the things she had taught me about sewing.

I felt elated at the thought—to have let go of the pain and yet to have remembered the good, to have drawn on Mamma's strength and her love for beauty. Perhaps I was really growing up despite Kelda's laments.

I flattened the last facing carefully, pinned the fabric snugly, and took the remaining pins from my mouth. "What do you think, Papa?" I stood back to look.

"About what, Annetti?"

"About these button loops, Papa. If there's one thing I hate, it's button loops, buttonholes, hooks and eyes. But you can hardly have clothes without some kind of fastener."

I stopped to wipe beads of sweat from my nose. The shop was hot and humid. For some reason, my nose always sweats more profusely than the rest of my face. I found the idiosyncrasy embarrassing, so I always kept a clean handkerchief in my pocket. Papa sometimes teased me about that, but he didn't even notice this time.

He came over for a closer inspection. "They look good. They do not look as if you hate them." He checked the markings and then smiled at me unexpectedly. "You will have to make yourself one next."

"A new suit for me, Papa? Do I need one? I have the brown wool dress Mamma made me last fall. It has lots of wear in it yet." I had secretly dreamed of suits from all those new wools, but I never even hoped to think that I might actually have one. Papa was not stingy with me, but he was frugal.

"*Ja*, sure," he replied thoughtfully. "You have clients now. They watch what you wear. What about that plum-colored wool? I saw you admiring it when you put the wools on the shelf."

I blushed at the fact that he had noticed and then threw my arms around his neck. "Oh, Papa, that would be wonderful, only—" A mischievous thought had popped into my head, and I pulled away from him slightly, my arms still about his neck. "You aren't trying to dress me up for buggy rides, are you? You aren't trying to get rid of me, are you?"

Papa laughed and laughed, but I never did receive an answer, for just then the little bells on the shop door tinkled as it opened. Papa turned as a small boy and his father entered.

"Well, what do you know? Nils and my little Dieter!" Papa shook Nils' hand and then knelt and held out his arms for Dieter, but the little boy walked slowly to him and only put his head on Papa's shoulder. Papa took Dieter's curly blond head gently in his hands and gazed into his sad blue eyes. "Tell Onkel Andrew where your smile went. Is it in your pocket? Tucked in your sleeve?" But Dieter was silent. "Did you swallow it?" Still no answer.

"You could talk last year when you were three. You told Onkel Andrew all about Cloquet and your Papa's mill. You came back to visit?"

"Papa—" I interrupted. I couldn't bear the agony of watching the hurt in Dieter's eyes and the serious gaze from Nils, who had always appeared a huge, incurably happy-go-lucky fellow.

My mind raced to explain the possibilities. It was his mother, my cousin Katrina, or the baby she was expecting—or both. Something drastically awful had happened, or they would not have come so unexpectedly all the way from Cloquet. I hadn't heard anything about their plans to visit. Surely I would have, if all were well.

"Papa," I repeated. "Dieter would like a cookie, I think. Wouldn't you, Dieter?" I waited until he slowly nodded his head. "Let's go upstairs and get one then. We'll get the whole jar and take it to the garden and watch the ants eat the crumbs."

I took his small hand in mine, and we walked silently through the back hall and up the stairs to the kitchen. I gave Dieter two tin cups to carry downstairs, while I took the cookie jar and a tin pitcher full of milk. We sat on the steps of the back porch eating, but after a while Dieter tired of my oatmeal cookies. He left a half-eaten one on the step and started poking around the garden.

I followed him down the narrow stone walk between the rows, letting him pick one tomato, one carrot, one sprig of parsley and chives and basil. At Mamma's patch of mint, I stopped, fingering the leaves. They were no longer in bloom, but the smell brought back memories of Mamma.

"Dieter," I spoke softly. "Smell the mint here." I broke off a leaf and held it under his nose. "These were my mother's favorite, especially when they bloomed. She used to make tea from these too." I stopped. I felt sweaty—more so than I had felt inside the shop, despite the fine breeze outside. I swallowed. Talking about Mamma was not easy, but I had to go on. "I—I don't have a mother anymore, Dieter. She died."

I was kneeling by the mint, and I glanced up to see his brow wrinkled and his lips puckered. "Where did she go?" he finally asked.

I paused and sighed. "Your Tante Karin is in heaven, Dieter. She scraped her elbow on something when she was cleaning the back room. She didn't think anything of it at first, but the wound became infected. It made her so sick she died. It was awful to see her hurt so, Dieter."

Dieter looked up at me with his big, round eyes. "Didn't *Bestefar* fix her? My mamma says our baby wouldn't have died if *Bestefar* had been there to help."

Tears sprang to my eyes. *So that's what happened!* I sighed and looked up at the fluffy clouds pushed across the sky by a stiff breeze, up where I tried to imagine heaven might be. "Your *bestefar* tried to help my mother, Dieter, but—well—I—I guess God had other plans."

Dieter fingered the mint plants a bit longer, smelled his hands, and smiled briefly at the fragrance. He looked up at me and paused before he asked, "Is it a nice place?" His little voice sounded so serious.

"What—heaven? I'm sure that it must be. I've heard the pastor say that the streets of heaven are made of gold, and there are mansions made special for us."

"Papa says our baby is in heaven now. Do they have people there to take care of little babies?" he persisted.

I nearly choked with tears. I knelt beside him and looked straight into his eyes. "My mamma would take care of your little baby. I'm sure of it, and there must be angels to take care of everyone too. I don't know, but I'll try to find out, Dieter. Would you like that?"

Dieter smiled a big smile and nodded. Impulsively, he threw his arms about me. *This must be what God's love feels like,* I marveled. *In the midst of sorrow springs joy. If only I'd had the simple trust of this child, I might have been spared months of misery.*

Nils appeared on the back step just then with Papa. He had opened his mouth to speak but stood staring at Dieter instead. A slow grin spread across his face. "Dieter, Onkel Andrew is going to measure you for new clothes just like mine. How about that, Dieter?"

Dieter smiled even bigger and ran to hug his father. Nils picked him up and swung him around in the air, set him down, ruffled his hair, and noisily kissed his nose. I watched with pleasure. Nils was a big, strapping fellow, the kind of man who could make you feel that all of life is smiling at you.

Papa chuckled while Nils grinned over at me. Dieter bent down to grab his cookie from the step, and Papa laughed outright. "Ho, ho! Look! The ants have found your cookie. They like it better than the crumbs, eh?"

Dieter nodded, brushed off the ants, and popped the rest of the cookie into his mouth.

Papa winked at me. "Now that is a real boy. Ants or no ants, the cookie is his! Well, big boy, what do you say we measure you?" Papa took Dieter by the hand and led him into the shop.

"All right, Onkel Andrew," Dieter replied.

Nils watched them, grinning, but made no move to follow. I grew uncomfortable with his presence. I knew that his baby had died, but I didn't know what to say without hurting him. And why would I want to remind him of sorrow, now that he seemed so happy? So I did nothing. I sighed lightly and knelt beside the patch of mint, watching a ladybug on one of the leaves.

"I have been trying to make him laugh or smile all the way from Cloquet. He has walked around with a drooping face ever since that awful night. I don't know what you said or did to make him smile, Annetti," Nils finally said, "but thank you a thousand times."

I blushed. I hardly knew what to think. "I—I'm sorry about the baby, Nils. Katrina must feel simply awful."

He sighed and sat down heavily on the step. "Yes. I hope that she'll be all right now—and not hate me for taking her to Cloquet. I don't want to leave her here, but I know that she'll get the best of care at home. If only I could talk Dr. Nelson into moving to Cloquet with us! The closest doctor is in Duluth, nearly twenty miles away."

I silently shuddered to think of Onkel Peter and Tante Janna moving so far away, but I said nothing of that. I looked at him in shock. "You're leaving Katrina and Dieter here?"

"I don't know what else to do. Life has not been easy in Cloquet. Business is growing, but the few families who could befriend us are struggling to survive themselves. I must work all day at keeping the mill running if I hope to provide for my family. And largely because of that, life is lonesome for Katrina."

He brightened then. "We started building a house, a big one on Carlton Avenue. I'm going to finish it before Katrina comes back. With work and all, finishing the house might take most of a year, but it will be good for Katrina to be with her parents in the meantime."

I smiled back at him. "A real house—with plaster walls?"

Nils nodded and grinned with pride.

I remembered the letters from Katrina that Tante Janna had read to Mamma when we visited. Cloquet seemed to be a town of small houses with tarpaper walls and small windows—nothing like Tante Janna and Onkel Peter's house, where Katrina had grown up.

"She'll love having a whole year to collect wallpaper and make curtains," I predicted. "And Tante Janna will buy her parlor furniture as a house-warming gift, I'll bet."

Nils laughed. "You make me feel better already, Annetti." Nils stood. "Thanks again for looking after Dieter."

I stood too, feeling the cramp in my legs at having squatted beside the mint for so long. "He's a sweet child, Nils—precocious, too. And he'll miss his father dearly."

"I'd be obliged if you and your father would help to look after him, Annetti. I fear for him in a house full of girls. He has always loved his Onkel Andrew, and you seem to understand what he needs."

"I'll be glad to try," I promised, gazing back at the patch of mint. It seemed strange to be the one to comfort others, but it was a pleasant change.

I listened to the hollow sound of his footsteps on the porch as he returned to the shop. Then, with a sigh, I picked up the bowl of cookies, the cups, and the empty pitcher of milk. I carried them upstairs. I took the bowl of cookies to the shop, thinking that Papa or Dieter might want a few more. Papa was kneeling behind the counter, measuring Dieter this way and that with his tape, muttering and jotting numbers on a scrap of paper. He winked at me when I entered. "Customer for you, Annetti."

I brushed past him with an eager smile on my lips, my eyes sweeping across the shop. They fell on a head of wavy golden hair. My customer was sitting in one of Mamma's side chairs browsing through *Godey's Lady's Book*. I nearly dropped the bowl of cookies. It was Lars! At the clatter of the bowl on the counter, he looked up. His face wore a sheepish grin.

I stood speechless for a moment, but I managed to collect my wits after a few shallow breaths. "And what can I do for you?" I asked stiffly. I don't know why I mimicked Papa's accent. It just came out that way.

"Your English, ma'am, is almost as bad as that of your father," he replied, his eyes twinkling merrily. I heard Papa choke down a laugh, and I could feel the flush of embarrassment creeping up my neck. "I came to collect that jar of blackberry jam that you promised me."

"I made no such promise," I remonstrated. "I merely stated that such a wish was a clever idea on your part."

Papa stood up just then and looked at me, then Lars, and back. A slow grin spread across his face. "Did you forget how to make jam, Annetti?" he asked teasingly.

I looked from him to Dieter to Nils behind me. They were all grinning. *They are scoundrels, all of them, to tease me so,* I thought defiantly. But most of all, I blamed Lars for having the audacity to walk into our busy shop and embarrass me like this. Oh, I was furious!

I straightened and turned to Lars, my eyes flashing and my voice brimming with cold courtesy. "Have a cookie instead, Reverend Sorenson. I have not had time to make jam. I have two orders to fill. Now, if you will excuse me—" I took the blue wool jacket from the dressmaking form and busied myself at the worktable sewing on buttons and loops.

From the corner of my eye, I saw Papa wink at Lars. "*Ja,* you will have to come back when we are not so busy."

That comment was too much for Nils. He laughed aloud, so Papa introduced him, and they talked about traveling and the lumber business and carpentry and Cloquet. I felt grateful that they were ignoring me, but it was hard for me to ignore them. Lars seemed quite interested in the young town, though I couldn't imagine why. Who would want to live in a tarpaper shack?

Dieter grew restless with all the talk, so I put down my work—despite the pretense of being busy—and took him back out to the garden. The day was so warm that I let him take off his shoes and socks, roll up his knickers, and splash around at the pump. After a while, I fetched a clean towel and dried his hands and feet. I was combing his hair back into place when Nils poked his head out the back door and called for him.

Dieter scampered to his father, but I didn't hurry back into the shop. A pleasant breeze fluttered the hollyhocks by the porch railing. I wandered through the garden and picked several fallen gladiola stalks to place in a vase on the counter. Then I headed back.

He was *still* there with Papa. They were talking about churches now. "I have stayed with Olin enough to visit," Lars was saying. "If I stay longer, I am sure to be in the way with Inga's baby coming and all. I want to go somewhere that has no church yet, but I have to go somewhere that also offers vurk."

Papa was nodding in assent. "Cloquet—she sounds like a booming town. I would not mind going there myself. Business is slow here now, except for Annetti's customers." Papa winked at me, but I didn't respond. I was alarmed by the idea of Papa wanting to move.

"Surely there are towns around here that don't have a church. Onkel Peter would know. He's been to nearly every town on the county map at the post office."

Lars and Papa both stared at me in astonishment.

"That is a good idea! I will go now," Lars exclaimed eagerly, and he started toward the door.

"If you get a chance, could you tell Dieter about heaven? I didn't know what to say."

He turned, his blue eyes questioning. "Of course! At your service, ma'am. Thank you for the cookies. I will return later for my jar of jam." He winked at Papa and was gone.

The afternoon was full of explanations. Of course, Papa was curious about the jam incident, but he seemed satisfied with the brief summary I gave him.

He was quiet for a long time after our talk. "You remind me of your mother, Annetti. I never understood why she did certain things." He sighed and continued. "I think he likes you. He's a fine young man. I would be honored to have him for a son-in-law. Perhaps that plum-colored wool suit is not the only thing you should make for yourself."

I was so stunned and embarrassed by his speech that I didn't say a word.

7: Faith or Fear

That evening, I heard about Lars' visit with Dr. Nelson in great detail. Kelda rehearsed the entire event to me at least once. She rattled on, full of excitement, as I listened quietly.

She had been working at Onkel Peter's apothecary shop adjacent to the clinic when Lars called. Onkel Peter was out on calls at the time. So of course she kept Lars well entertained until his return. She filled him with descriptions of the many towns to which Dr. Nelson had traveled. Having occasionally accompanied her father, she could tell stories nearly as well as Onkel Peter did—-stories of the Scotch family in Washburn attacked by a bear, of the smallpox outbreak in Sanborn or the diphtheria plague of 1885.

I had no such fascinating stories, no captivating blue eyes. I wondered if Lars would forget about the blackberry jam due to obvious attractions. How could he not help being attracted to Kelda's striking beauty? His first wife had been beautiful, so beautiful.

Remembering how plain I looked in comparison, I felt let-down. I was glad I had not dared to believe Papa's wild speculations. What did Papa know? If it were true that Lars liked me, the man would tell me himself. Well, okay. He had told me he liked me, but "like" is not "love." I felt distant from all the excitement, but I listened and smiled appropriately at Kelda's enthusiasm. After all, she was my cousin, and she was indeed beautiful. How could I deny her the joy that fed my grief?

Kelda had given Lars the grand tour of Onkel Peter's clinic and apothecary, where she worked afternoons mixing up tonics and whatnot for Onkel Peter. She happened to mention that they needed a locked cabinet in which to store the medicines, now that Dieter had come to stay. Dieter had already drunk half a bottle of Onkel Peter's cough elixir, the one sweetened with honey. They didn't dare to leave the medicines on the open shelves as before, even if the apothecary shop was forbidden territory for Dieter.

When Onkel Peter returned, Kelda had convinced him to pay Lars to build a cabinet. So Lars had work to do. He was to start Monday, after making arrangements to stay in town.

Papa heard all of this conversation too, since he had been sweeping the shop when Kelda arrived. I was thankful that he didn't wink at me or let on that Lars had been here first. He didn't say anything afterward, and I wondered what he thought of Kelda's chatter. Little did I know Papa had plans of his own.

We were in church the following Sunday. I had worn my white lawn dress with the sprigs of lavender flowers, but I felt warm, very warm, despite the sheer fabric. I had just used my handkerchief to blot the beads of sweat from my nose and had turned to Papa to comment on the unbearable heat in the pews that morning, when Papa grinned at me and winked.

"Papa!" I whispered in exasperation, supposing he was teasing me about my sweaty nose. But he had turned from me and was nodding hello to Olin and Inga. Then he stood to shake hands with Lars and continued talking with him in front of everyone, much to my dismay.

Embarrassment crept into me as I recalled Papa's choice for a son-in-law. I had to remind myself that others had no inkling of such wild and crazy ideas. After all, they were talking quietly about "vurking" and ignoring me. But I nearly choked when Papa invited him to dinner.

Papa feigned surprise: "What is the matter, Annetti? Did you not clean well enough for company?"

I was glad that the worship service started then, giving me an excuse for no reply. I had a hard time concentrating on Pastor Lyndahl's sermon that morning, to say the least. All I could think of was dinner. I had not fixed anything fancy, as Tante Janna always did when she had company. I had put a pot of baked beans and bacon in the oven, along with a pan of steamed brown bread with raisins. There would be plenty of both, but it was simple fare—nothing compared to Tante Janna's fine dinners. And for dessert? Tante Janna always served dessert on Sundays. There would not be time for me to make much of anything.

I glanced over at Papa, wondering if any of these culinary worries had even occurred to him. He sat listening to the sermon so intently that I wondered what I was missing. Then a panic swept through me. Lars would be interested in a sermon, of course, and if he were coming to dinner, surely the sermon would be one topic of conversation. Not wanting to appear ignorant, I forced myself to pay attention.

I had at least opened Mamma's Bible to the New Testament text, Romans 8:28. I carefully re-read the verse: "All things work together for good to those who love God...." Pastor Lyndahl, in his calm, quiet voice, was speaking about Elijah. At first I did not see the connection with the text. The anger of the wicked King Ahab and the three-year, nationwide drought—how could those things work any good? But he pointed out God's goodness to Elijah through the drought. Elijah had food and water at the brook, and when that dried up, God miraculously displayed His love and power at the widow's home.

There were undoubtedly many truths too deep for me to grasp that morning, but I caught the glimmer of one truth. It both amazed me and made me hunger for more: the truth that God directs the circumstances of our everyday lives—that even hardships have a purpose in His plan. I wished I had listened more carefully to the Old Testament text, something about "plans for good, to prosper you." Perhaps Lars would mention it at dinner, and I could read it for myself.

I dabbed the sweat off my nose and forehead as we stood for the closing hymn. The day was warm—a great day for ice-cold lemonade. Lemons were a luxury for us, but Tante Janna might have some. I thought of asking to borrow some, but I quickly dismissed that idea. Papa never wanted to be beholden to anyone, especially relatives. If I wanted a cold drink to serve, it would have to be ice water. At least we did have ice. I could chop a chunk off the block in the ice chest, which we kept in the cellar. I would put it in an old sugar sack and pound it to bits. We could have plenty of ice water, I thought pleasantly.

A sudden hush brought me back to my senses. Pastor Lyndahl was praying. I bowed my head quickly but not quick enough to miss the curl of a smile on Papa's lips.

"About what were you thinking?" he teased me afterward, loudly enough for Lars to hear as he came over to join us.

"Papa!" I pleaded in a hushed tone. I could see the teasing twinkle in Papa's eyes and the amused curiosity in Lars' eyes. *How very much alike their eyes look,* I thought. The similarity was uncanny. After a moment of reluctant silence, I gave Papa a little embarrassed smile. "A glass of cold ice water, Papa."

I remember clearly Lars' laugh—that clear, deep, ringing tone I had heard the first day we met. Papa looked at Lars in question. "I was too," he choked out between laughs. He was laughing at himself. Then Papa started in. Together they laughed so loudly that everyone turned to see what was so funny. Amazingly, I did not care. I stood grinning back at Papa and Lars, amused for a change. The whole situation was ridiculous. We had come to church for spiritual instruction, and all we could think of was the mundane—even Lars, the preacher. For the first time I realized that humor wasn't a matter of jokes. It involved how one looked at life.

Afterward, we stood in the churchyard and visited with Olin, Inga, and Adelle. Kelda paraded over with a big smile on her face. "*Mor* would like for all of you to come and have dinner with us today. We're having standing rib roast and apple pie."

I watched her vivacious expression uneasily, my heart sinking. I had begun to look forward to our dinner, despite the plain fare. I was excited to have time with Lars. Now that time would have to be shared. Kelda would dominate any conversation involving Lars. Papa would never ask him again, I was sure. We hardly ever had company.

For a moment everyone was silent. Olin looked at Inga, and then put his arm around her. "Thank you, but I think I need to take my wife home. She is exhausted with the heat."

"I think Inga will need me too," Adelle added. "But it was so kind of you to ask."

"It is terribly hot," Kelda conceded with a smile, her glance turned toward Papa and Lars. I felt my heart climb into my throat. Papa smiled but said nothing. It seemed that we were expected to join the Nelsons whenever they offered.

Finally Lars spoke. "Thank you very much. You are kind to invite me again. I would, in fact, love to join you—"

My throat suddenly ached, and I could feel a tear gathering in the corners of my eyes.

"Good," Kelda interrupted happily.

"*Nei*—I mean I would love to join you today, but today I cannot."

Kelda looked surprised. I was glad that Lars had not told her why, but when she looked at me, I wondered if she suspected that I knew why. "I would love for you all to come," she said pleasantly, looking directly at me, as if she expected me to encourage a decision in her favor.

I felt trapped. I did not want her to find out Papa had invited Lars to dinner with us, and I did not want to give up dinner with him, but if I didn't say something in Kelda's favor, she would ask me why later. "You wouldn't want to miss Tante Janna's standing rib roast," I suggested. "And the first apples of the season make delicious pie."

Kelda smiled gloriously at that, and her now-hopeful gaze shifted to Lars. He shook his golden head, however. "I thank you. But tell your *mor* that I would love to come some other time."

I watched Kelda's eyebrows arch in surprise, but she forced a pleasant smile and shrugged good-naturedly. I knew how much she wanted him to accept the invitation, and I admired her self-control. As for myself, I was relieved and yet disappointed that there would be "some other time." It didn't seem as if I had gained much.

We walked home in the heat. Papa stayed in the shop parlor with Lars while I went up to the kitchen. The heat there was nearly unbearable. Since our shop had no trees nearby, the sun hit it full force. Along with the heat of the oven all morning, the kitchen was not a fit place to work, much less to eat, even with the windows open.

I weighed the alternatives thoughtfully. We could eat in the parlor downstairs, where it was somewhat cooler, though sitting around the counter might be somewhat awkward. Or we could—that was it! We could go on a picnic. I knew just the spot too.

Quickly, I lined a wicker clothesbasket with newspapers and placed the pot of beans and steaming brown bread inside. I covered them with more newspaper in case of spills and tucked an old quilt on top. I dumped the clothespins out of a smaller wicker basket and packed spoons and bowls, a knife, butter, glasses, blue gingham napkins, and several ripe tomatoes from the vines in the back yard. Then I raced to the cellar with a large glass jar and the tools for chipping ice.

I heard Papa shouting down the cellar steps several minutes later. "Annetti, what is all this racket?"

"Just a moment, Papa," I called. Quickly, I emptied the sugar sack full of crushed ice into a huge old pickle jar and headed up the steps with my treasure. I handed him the jar. "It's the sound of a picnic lunch, complete with ice water," I replied, brushing my cold hands gingerly across the skirt of my dress.

"Picnic?" Papa looked at me, dumbfounded, while Lars laughed.

"Papa, it's like an oven upstairs. Give Lars the jar. He can add water from the pump out back. I need your help upstairs with the basket."

We sat in the shade on the grassy shoreline overlooking the bay. I had come to this spot many times as a child, but I hadn't visited it since Mamma's death. How good to feel again the wisps of breeze brushing against my face! To listen to the soothing lap of the water and stare at the dull blue-gray line where the Superior met the sky! Coming back to this spot was like greeting an old friend. A rush of good memories embraced me.

We spent a wonderful afternoon there. Despite the simple fare, Lars seemed to enjoy the meal, and I was glad that I had listened to the sermon. Lars seemed to find depths of wisdom that I'd missed, and it dawned on me that perhaps all this time, the cause of boredom had been my obstinate attitude.

The Old Testament passage I'd missed had come from Jeremiah 29, pronounced by the weeping prophet, Lars said: "I know the plans that I have for you, plans to prosper you and not for calamity, to give you a future and a hope." I thought about that verse as I cleaned up our picnic. I could see how God had prospered Onkel Peter and even Nils and Katrina despite the loss of their child. Olin, Inga, Adelle, and the farm were prospering marvelously. But Papa and me—how could Mamma's death be anything but tragic?

"You look so serious," Lars remarked.

"That complaint," I stated matter-of-factly, "has been noted before."

Papa just laughed.

"But there must be a reason," Lars countered. "On a beautiful day like this, surrounded by those who love you—?"

I looked up at him sharply. "You could hardly call Mamma's death anything but a calamity. She's not here. God may be prospering everyone else, but not us—not me." I took a deep breath and waited for his response.

"O ye of little faith!" Lars said—only his "faith" came out more like "fate."

"If we could always see the way God vurks, would we be asked to trust, to belief?"

His words stung me, but my fears struggled toward hope, for behind his words I heard the echo of Adelle's voice ringing through my mind: "God loves you, Annetti—you. Do you believe that?" I felt ashamed.

"You have a long walk back to Olin's farm tonight," Papa commented. He turned to Lars. "Annetti will have to pack you a supper. I wish I had a horse and wagon to give you a ride."

"I will enjoy the walk. I will not make it as often after I move to town."

"*Ja*, we understood from Kelda that you were going to move to town and start some carpentry vurk for them. Where will you stay?" Papa asked.

"I talked with Widow Thompson this morning. She has a room I can rent. She will let me pay by fixing up the roof and the fence in the yard, perhaps other things. I will have to find somewhere to eat meals, though. I was starting to worry about that, when the pastor spoke a good lesson in faith. I think—I think this is a way for my faith to grow. I can learn to trust that God vurks all things together for good." He turned to me. "You see, my faith must grow too. We help each other, *ja*?"

"You can eat with us," Papa offered. "Unless you think Annetti's cooking is no good. Maybe she will even remember how to make jam." A smile curled on Papa's lips.

I stiffened at the playful jab. *There were certain things I would be a fool to believe.*

Papa ignored my silence and went on. "As for a carpentry shop where you can vurk, we have a back room that is empty—"

"Papa!" I interrupted with a tone of horror. "Not that awful back room! You know how I feel about it." I felt the flush of embarrassment creeping up my neck. To have my weaknesses, my fear and impulsive outburst displayed before Lars brought me shame. How I longed for Kelda's polite restraint!

Papa looked at me with sad eyes. "Annetti, it is time that we filled that room with some good memories."

I swallowed hard, struggling to harness my emotions. "Don't, Papa! It's full of nothing but bad luck. How could you wish that on anyone, especially Lars?"

My eye caught the flicker of Lars' smile.

"Annetti, when all things vurk together for good, there is not any room for such a thing as bad luck."

"Then what do you call tragedy?" I countered, almost bitter.

"I call it the will of God, the opportunity for faith to grow, faith in the truth that God loves you and will take care of you." No crinkles creased the corners of his blue eyes now. Their calmness held me nonetheless.

I bit my lip.

He paused and looked steadily at me. "*Ja*, I know that is easy for me to say, now that I have the offer of a room to vurk—but will you trust God?"

I smiled weakly but deigned no reply.

"I will pray for you," he promised, patting my arm.

I breathed a light sigh. "Why is it that one can understand and agree with a whole sermon, yet believing it in life is so difficult?"

"Hamartiology," Lars answered. I didn't even ask. And I was secretly glad that no one noticed the lack of dessert.

8: Scheming Fathers and the Parade

Papa and Lars talked about the old country on our walk back to the shop, recalling long hikes through the mountains, holiday celebrations, and—of all things—pickled fish. *Lutefisk*. I had never given much thought to how different life was here for Papa. Mamma and Papa had never talked about the old country, as far as I could remember. I wondered how much I didn't know about Papa. Sometime I would ask, I promised myself.

As it turned out, Lars did not come for several weeks. He cleared land for Olin, cutting down trees and burning out stumps. In return, Olin let him keep the best lumber for his own use. When Lars finally did move to town, he ate only breakfasts and suppers with us at first.

We settled into a pleasant routine. Every morning shortly after daybreak, he would rap briskly at the back porch door. Papa would let him in, and then I would hear the whistling of some nondescript melody—his "hungry tune" I called it—and a heavy stomp up the stairs. At first I had wondered why his footsteps sounded so heavy, until I noticed that the wood-box beside the stove was always full now, a pleasure for which I thanked him often.

Papa began teasing me about the breakfasts that I fixed. "What is it this morning, Annetti? I always have to wonder what I eat for breakfast, now that Lars comes. Is it flapjacks or muffins or porridge or sweet rolls or fruit soup? More than likely it is some other concoction."

"Papa, I told you last night that we were having toasted cinnamon bread this morning. I don't know why you can't remember."

"*Ja*, but you do not know how much trouble it is to have to remember," he complained with a chuckle. "It is plain unsettling."

"*Ja*," Lars winked at me. "I think it worries him, what he will eat, but he has no trouble eating, I notice."

Even Papa laughed at that. Sometimes I thought Papa's carrying on was an underhanded scheme to compliment my cooking, but I was never quite sure. To be true, I had not taken many pains before to put variety into our menu. But I took this meal business seriously, and it seemed natural to put more thought into quality.

Since Lars spent mornings and some of the afternoon of the first few weeks repairing Widow Thompson's roof and porch steps and fence, I packed him a generous lunch—always with something fresh from the garden. Usually it was simple: potato salad in a bowl of lettuce leaves, a dish of cottage cheese with chives, thick slices of bread and butter with sausage and tomatoes, and always a jar of ice water.

He asked me to continue packing a lunch even when he started working all day in the back room. He seemed to enjoy eating one meal alone. Perhaps he sensed that Papa and I needed time alone too. He usually sat on the back porch and read as he ate. Then, craving exercise, he would go for a short walk along the lake before returning to his work.

His evenings too were spent working on the cabinet for the Nelsons. I frequently brought him a cup of hot tea and cookies late in the evening, knocking at the doorway to the back room, hesitant to enter the room of ill memory. At first he would stand near the doorway and talk while he ate. Sometimes he coaxed me to have the faith to overcome my fear of stepping inside.

Sometimes I ventured so far as to sit and watch him, noting how he bored holes for the locks or filed the edges until the lock fit snugly. I felt shy; I knew little worth sharing, so I rarely talked. Lars, seeming to prefer the comfort of amiable chatter as he worked, often kept up my side of the conversation in addition to his.

"If you are wondering why I chose this piece of wood," he would begin in Norwegian—and then go on to explain how each different wood had a distinctive grain and use. "Maybe you ask why I notch the ends of these boards," he would venture, providing a detailed description of how he planned to fit and glue a drawer.

One day he startled me by looking up abruptly and fastening his eyes on me. "You are not like most women," he stated. "You do not talk much."

"I can talk plenty when I have something worth saying," I answered simply, not knowing whether his remark constituted criticism, admiration, or mere observation.

He arched his eyebrow at that, but he didn't comment.

His silence seemed uncomfortable, so I tried to justify my behavior. "Some day, I will have gathered enough wisdom to know what to say. I will be wise, like your mother."

"Why my mother?" he asked, scrutinizing me all of a sudden.

"Because she is the one who taught me how to believe," I said. He remained silent, with a surprised look on his face, so I told him what happened that day at the farm, about how Adelle had cared to help me and how I had admired her confidence.

"More lies behind the demeanor of a quiet woman than one expects," he mumbled in Norwegian when I had finished. I wasn't sure whether he meant me or his mother; I still considered myself a girl, not a woman. I didn't respond.

Another day, I finally mustered the courage to ask him about his walks along the lakeshore. "To whom do you speak?" I asked. "I have often wondered."

"I had no idea that anyone was watching," he replied, without answering directly.

"I see you sometimes from the upstairs window. You seem to be talking to someone, but nobody is there."

"Well," he chuckled good-naturedly. "I am not old enough to be talking to myself."

I smiled and waited for him to go on.

"I talk to God, Annetti," he answered seriously.

"What do you say?"

"Whatever I desire or worry about," he answered. "I tell Him exactly how I feel, and I beg His help and advice. Sometimes I even remind God of His promises."

"Is that the same as praying?" I asked.

His blue eyes crinkled at the corners as he smiled. "*Ja.*"

I learned to feel comfortable in his presence. My curiosity won out over my reticence, and I looked forward to his answers to my questions. As he slowly shaped the cabinet from raw materials into a lovely piece, so he gradually reformed my memories of the room. I came to treasure the companionship and creative industry it represented. The pleasure didn't endure, however.

We seemed to be having an increasing number of customers who came to browse through the shop. Never before had Mamma experienced such interest in fashion. Most of her clientele had arrived without flourish, eager to have her fill specific orders. They devoured *Godey's Lady's Book* mostly while they sat waiting for some alteration to be completed.

Now, many of the visitors never placed an order until they had poured over several issues countless times. True, clothing trends seemed to be changing rapidly: Hoops were going out of fashion, while bustles were coming into fashion. Then too, the wardrobes of Ashland's summer residents had begun to reflect an opulence they had not previously possessed, and the daring color combinations intrigued Ashland's otherwise conservative crowd.

I certainly did not dare to think that my skills as a seamstress excelled Mamma's. I began to suspect that some other reason explained the traffic.

Inevitably, during my customers' browsing process, I would have to explain the reason for the steady sawing or pounding or sanding in the back room. My clientele would poke their heads in and admire the shell of the Nelson's new cabinet. They would linger for a friendly chat with Lars before suddenly remembering that they simply must stop by the milliner's shop to examine the latest in fall hats or check the cobbler's shop for the latest in boots. To me, their visits seemed contrived.

Lars gained orders from the traffic. Mrs. Hannah Tucker, who kept the books at her husband's dry goods store down the street, decided she wanted a writing desk and captain's chair large enough to accommodate her enormous width. Then the fashionable Eustacia Hotchkiss wanted a footstool for the embroidered cushion she had nearly finished.

A rash of women pounced on an old idea bandied about with a new name. They ordered "hope chests," cedar-lined trunks in which their daughters would store the linens made in hope of marrying and starting their own households. Even Tante Janna ordered one for Kirsten, a decision that gave Kelda yet another reason to stop by nearly every morning.

Kelda always brought Dieter with her, a good pretext for a longer visit since Dieter, curious about everything, asked a thousand questions. Lars would put him to work sanding a drawer knob or a rounded leg. Dieter thrived with such attention, begging us to feel how smooth the object was now. Inevitably, I would have to stop working and fetch a bowl of cookies and a pot of tea or pitcher of milk because they stayed so long.

I benefited from the extra traffic. My work came in floods. I had no sooner finished the blue wool suits for the twins than I had another big order, dresses for Anna and Trina Larson. Their Sunday dresses had been worn so thin that I hated to think how their everyday dresses looked. Their father Gus had brought them in to be measured for two winter dresses apiece, but I cut my price and made them each three. Like me, they had no mother.

Tante Janna came to order winter dresses for Kirsten, who was growing like a weed. Widow Thompson came in to order a fashionable Sunday dress. Her roof and fence had been fixed, and she seemed both excited and thankful to have rent money to spend on herself. Hers was my first order for an older woman. Soon afterward, the wife of the man who managed the Chequamegon Hotel placed a substantial order for finery.

Think of that, Annetti! Your work will be on display at Ashland's affluent lakeshore resort. I smiled at my success. I was building a reputation as a seamstress of style. I wondered to myself whether Widow Thompson had a wider circle of gossiping friends than we knew, whether I had her to thank for my advertising boon.

I did not recognize the cause of our steady stream of browsing customers until the afternoon when I overheard two ladies from Washburn discussing their ailments. They launched into a lengthy conversation on the marvels of a new headache powder and the proposed treatment for hot flashes. I had heard the very same conversation countless times over, but the significance hadn't clicked until now. I choked down a giggle, and Papa—who had been fiddling about uncomfortably with little to do—shot me a stern, questioning stare.

"And what was so funny today?" Papa demanded afterwards. "To laugh at the customers is not a good idea."

That night at supper, he brought up the subject again, and this time I made no attempt to stifle my amusement. I grinned and arched my eyebrows.

"Well?"

"I've been wondering what started the parade to the back room," I explained.

"Parade?"

"What else would you call it? You yourself have complained about the stream of gabbing women who do little but gawk and distract us from our work."

"And?"

"Well, you know. We seem to have developed a new clientele. They make a pretense of poring over Mamma's magazines, yet they do more looking than ordering—and more chattering than that. Then they all seem curious about the noise in the back room. It's as if they already know about Lars and just come to look."

"Annetti—" Papa reprimanded, glancing at Lars.

"But that's what they are doing, Papa, and I just figured out why. It's Onkel Peter! You know how Tante Janna always teases him about how he puts his patients at ease with a little small talk—'Nothing but the latest gossip,' she says."

"This time the gossip just happens to be a handsome bachelor in whom his daughter has a sharp interest, and all the scheming mothers and old-lady matchmakers have to see for themselves." I faltered and glanced at Lars, blushing at having admitted to his face that he was handsome. He was blushing!

"I fail to see what is so funny," Papa commented flatly.

"Can't you imagine Onkel Peter slapping his knee and having a jolly laugh over the results of his stories? He distracts his patients' attention from their ailments by telling them about Kelda's latest infatuation. They complain about how debilitating their symptoms are, but they manage a rapid recovery. They think his new headache powder is wonderful, but it's not that at all that prompts them to go out visiting. It's the curiosity of gossip. They simply must check to see if Lars is as charming a man as Onkel Peter paints in his stories. You know how he loves to exaggerate!"

Papa frowned sternly at me again.

"Oh, Papa! I love you dearly, but sometimes you are ever so clueless. My biggest worry is that I'll have to start paying Lars a commission for every new order I take on."

Lars' face broke into a wide grin. "The old rascal!" he complained affably. "The only thing is, now that you tell me, these scheming mothers will worry me."

"Oh, I wouldn't be afraid of any scheming mothers, if I were you," I assured him. "I'd worry a great deal more over the scheming fathers." I had meant Onkel Peter; I realized my gaffe when Papa cleared his throat and announced the need to inventory the fabrics.

"Thanks for the advice." Lars winked at me as he too stood up to leave.

I blushed and started to clear the table. Washing up the dishes, I realized I may have made a huge gaffe. I had disclosed to Lars that Kelda found him irresistible. Would that change how he felt about her?

Lately we'd had more 'back-room visitors' than we had for Mamma's funeral. Strange how I no longer dreaded the back room, how the mention of Mamma no longer sent a piercing pain to my heart. Thoughts of her were all around me, but they had become comforting thoughts.

Mamma! How different would my life be now if you had lived? Would Papa have rented the back room to Lars? I couldn't picture Mamma as one of those scheming mothers. Truthfully, I sometimes had trouble picturing her at all. I thought of the dream I had last night. Mamma had seemed so real. I had been trying to tell her about Lars, but she didn't understand. She kept saying that she couldn't think of who he was.

Despite Lars' growing orders and my mounting work, Papa's work was not thriving. He had made a few outfits for Dieter, but he only had one order after that—an extra shirt for Pastor Lyndahl, one with a stiff clerical collar. I knew Papa wouldn't charge for that, and I hated to think of how restless he would be when he finished.

But surprisingly, he wasn't restless. He started in on a whole wardrobe of heavy canvas trousers and plaid flannel shirts and—of all things—union suits. I had not seen such an order written in the ledger book, and it puzzled me. I did not dare to ask. All he said once when I looked at him quizzically was, "Annetti, I do not want you to forget about that plum-colored suit for yourself. When you have customers, you have to look sharp."

"I hardly have time now, Papa," I reminded him.

"*Ja*, but when you get a minute free, you start." And he tried on the shirt to which he had just stitched the cuffs. He had often tried on his orders, even if the size did not match his. He claimed it helped him figure the right proportions, but I never had any luck with his method. I stuck purely to my measuring tape on that point.

The shirt hung in folds at Papa's armpits. The cuffs fell down past his fingertips. Obviously, he was not sewing for himself. For whom, then? The question puzzled me.

9: Papa and His "Vurk"

It is definitely tea weather, I thought as I picked up the jacket to Widow Thompson's new outfit and started hemming. I stared out the shop window after one of my new "browsing" customers. *One of those cold, gray November days—Mamma's 'tea weather,'* I mused. I had begun keeping hot tea on the pot-bellied stove in the shop, and whenever customers came to browse, I would offer them a cup.

I was not as good as Mamma had been about drawing their conversation toward the gossip of fashion and commenting on how remarkably good or stylish each looked in a certain color or cut. I felt somewhat awkward, not wanting to sound pushy or insincere. I mostly listened, hoping that as my experience grew, my customers would ask for my opinion.

Papa used to complain teasingly to Mamma that she could have finished five orders in the time she spent visiting with her customers. "*Ja,*" she would reply good-naturedly. "And I have ten more orders because I do visit."

Papa never teased me about that, however, perhaps because I frequently stood at the counter and worked while I listened. Or was it because he did not want to be reminded of his lack of orders?

Supper had become an event to which we all looked forward. The meal itself was a simple affair, a leisurely meal of bread and cheese or potato soup or rice cooked in milk and served with butter, cinnamon, and sugar. At first Lars had eaten quietly and returned to the back room. He would work evenings and then leave for Widow Thompson's.

Gradually he and Papa talked more and more, starting in their broken English and slipping into Norwegian as they reminisced about the old country. As the weather grew colder, Lars didn't return as often to the chilly back room. He would stay and help Papa dry the dishes, and they would talk about lessons in character and faith.

One evening I asked Lars to look up that passage about "plans to prosper." He read me Jeremiah 29:11. I felt again the thrill of God's love, the thrill of believing His goodness to me, of growing in faith and knowledge. Papa felt the thrill too, I think, for he began asking Lars to read a certain passage of Scripture every night.

So began the winter evenings, November and December when darkness fell early. Lars would sit by the stove, his feet propped up on another chair, and read through the Psalms or the Gospels or Isaiah or Job. Papa would sit in Mamma's rocker with his cup of steaming tea, rocking slowly and listening intently. I would sit at the table, knitting while I listened.

I loved hearing the pleasant flow of words. The beauty of certain passages haunted me and drew me to pour over the verses later, when I was snuggled under my quilts. I would repeat the words to myself until I knew them by heart and felt the music of the phrases. My romance with the Scriptures consumed many late hours. Not even Lars was aware of the wisdom and strength I drank in long draughts, for I didn't talk of it.

I was sitting, enjoying his reading one evening, when he surprised me with a comment. "That is a wonderful much knitting you do. I think you never stop vurking."

I smiled at his English, thinking about our first meeting and my embarrassing rendition of "we dumb Norwegians have to vurk." A smile played on my lips, but I spoke nothing of that.

"Christmas knitting," I replied. "Tante Janna hosts a large family dinner every Christmas. They always have a tree that touches the ceiling, and sometimes Onkel Peter has to cut off the top to make it fit. There's never a bare spot underneath that tree. I expect there will be more than ever this year, with Katrina and Dieter at home."

I smiled. "Dieter will come off as royally as Kirsten. And there will be something nice for me too. I'd like to give them something in return."

Mamma had always taken care of making gifts for Tante Janna's celebration, but now this duty fell to me. I thought of all the colorful sweaters I had planned, using the complicated pattern of reindeer and snowflakes I had found tucked away in one of Mamma's sewing machine drawers. I had figured a way to reduce and adapt the design to mittens and scarves and caps and stockings. I had been busy knitting sets for Onkel Peter, Papa, and Dieter. I had started one for Lars too, after I noticed how shabby his coat looked hanging on the hooks by the back door.

"*Ja*," Lars replied thoughtfully. "I think I make something too—something for Olin and Inga and that little nephew of mine."

By this time, Lars had finished Onkel Peter's locked medicine cabinet as well as a few other orders. Kirsten's trunk was not yet finished, but Lars started another project regardless, one with many spindles. He would bring the spindles to the pot-bellied stove in our sewing area, since Papa was worried about Lars working in the cold. He even brought the spindles up evenings to work on after supper. I wondered what he was making until one evening I saw him boring holes into a long shaft and checking the spindles for fit. I was at the table braiding bread dough for a special breakfast. Papa had gone outside on a short errand.

"It's a crib!"

"*Ja*," he answered, looking up with a smile. "On Sunday I hear Inga tell all the things what that little rascal they have now does. I think it will not be long before he crawls out of that cradle. He is growing big!"

I smiled at the affection in his voice and on his face. "*Ja*," I remarked. "I've noticed how you keep up with the little fellow, begging Inga to hold him every Sunday and cooing over him until he gurgles with laughter. I expect you would know."

He gave me a silly smile. "You think I am a fool," he complained with a grin. "You will see. I will make a good father someday."

I blushed and wiped a smudge of flour off my cheek with my wrist. "Oh?" I remarked, arching my brows, "And is kissing babies something you learned in seminary too?"

He laughed—that deep musical laugh. It had grown to be a pleasant sound to my ears.

Later that evening, Papa and Lars sat by the stove sampling the little braided loaves I had made with scraps of tomorrow's breakfast bread. I was knitting again, concentrating on counting stitches as I switched colors. Lars and Papa had been talking softly. I had not paid attention to their conversation, but I looked up after a long silence. Both Papa and Lars were watching me. I looked at them questioningly.

"So," Lars stated with a note of finality. "What do you think?"

I looked at him, unsure of what he meant. "About what?"

"Cloquet."

His sudden attention unnerved me somewhat. I hid behind the guise of nonchalance: I shrugged and continued knitting. "What is there to think? It's just another small town."

Lars smiled at me patiently. "Of living there?"

I felt my heart jerk. *Was he going to live there? Why was he asking me what I thought, and why would my thoughts matter?*

Ever since I spoke of Kelda's infatuation, Lars' interest in her had blossomed. Oh, he was courteous enough at home, when only Papa and I were around. But even then, he often seemed oblivious to my presence. The cozy chats we shared had dwindled. Yet I noticed Lars could converse plenty when Kelda entered the room. Whenever she was there, I didn't seem to exist.

The thought hurt me, but I dared not reveal my true feelings. "It's not Ashland," I said finally. "I like Ashland. Dieter likes Cloquet, but I suppose that's because he spent most of his years there. I've spent most of mine here."

"*Ja,*" he considered. "To some, the life they know seems infinitely better than unknown adventure."

"You were born in Norway and spent most of your life there. What possessed you to leave and come here?" I asked. "Adventure to the unknown?"

"No, the dream of family and a better life—and of souls who would need to hear the Word of God."

I considered his answer for a moment. *Family? His brother's family or one of his own making?* I turned to Papa. "And you, Papa—why did you leave the old country?"

"Vurk."

"Of course," I replied, smiling fondly at him. The discussion ended there. I was left wondering why the subject of Cloquet had been raised.

I lay in bed that night, thinking over the question Lars had posed. Thank goodness that Papa hadn't done the asking! Ashland was my life—the shop, our little church, Onkel Peter and Tante Janna's home. I could not picture living anywhere else, away from the beauty of Lake Superior, away from the grassy spot where I had spent many dreamy hours, away from Mamma's grave.

Who would take care of Mamma's grave? I could never leave here! And yet Papa had left the place where he was born, where his parents were probably buried. He had left to look for work.

The dawning parallel disturbed me. Papa had no work here now. I shuddered beneath my quilts, sick at heart.

10: Christmas without Mamma

Christmas arrived far sooner than I had ever wanted. I had finished all the sweater sets and stuffed a mattress for the crib Lars was finishing, all the while agonizing over what to give Tante Janna, Katrina, Kelda, and Kirsten. They had everything, as far as I could see. Papa would never want me to spend money on the things I thought they would enjoy—jewelry or painted vases.

I would have to make something with the materials I had, but what? I settled on dressy cambric aprons with a simple tatted lace sewn along the edges. I had stayed up late every night the last week before Christmas to finish them.

Tante Janna had invited us to Christmas dinner, as usual. She had invited Lars too, but he had declined, promising that he would help clean up the leftovers the day after, if Onkel Peter and Papa would leave some of her "wonderful food."

On the afternoon of Christmas Eve, Onkel Peter volunteered to drive Lars out to the farm. I helped him strap the crib to the back of the sleigh. I had rolled up the mattress, with its cheerful cotton ticking, and tucked it inside the cage formed by the bars. I hadn't told Lars I was packing a present for him too. I had wrapped the sweater set carefully in brown paper and tied the package with a string. "For Lars" the package read; it didn't say from whom.

At the last minute I remembered Adelle. She wasn't my relative, but she had meant something special to me. "What can I give her?" I wondered. "An apron?" I hurried back inside and pulled out the apron I had made for Katrina. My eyes measured it carefully. Yes, it would work for Adelle. But what would I give Katrina then? I'd have to race through another apron.

Quickly I wrapped the package, this one labeled "For Adelle," and tucked it inside the crib with the mattress. I did not stay to see Lars and Onkel Peter off.

Tante Janna's Christmas Eve dinner could not have tasted more wonderful. I had come a little later than Papa had, having rushed with Katrina's gift. I had offered to help with the meal, but Tante Janna had assured me that she and Katrina could handle everything. For a change, I sat and enjoyed myself, though I sat next to Dieter and kept him entertained.

As always, Tante Janna served a feast. The table was loaded with dishes of candied sweet potatoes, escalloped corn, and baked cinnamon apples; platters of roast duck and savory ham; an urn of creamed peas; a boat of ham and milk gravy; plates of glazed meatballs; bowls of buttery mashed potatoes and steaming golden brown rolls.

"There's more food on this table than I could eat in a month," I thought to myself pleasantly. I thought of Lars, who would undoubtedly be enjoying a very traditional Norwegian meal with his family rather than Tante Janna's fashionable spread. I wondered which he would like better.

I had offered to clear the plates so that Tante Janna could enjoy her coffee and mincemeat pie when we heard a sharp rap at the door. Onkel Peter frowned and sighed. "I wonder who that would be, sick or hurt on Christmas Eve."

Reluctantly, he rose and headed for the front door. We heard him fling it open, and we felt the cold draft from the hall. "This is a surprise! Oh, but the snow! How did you come all this way? Here, I'll brush you off. Janna, set another plate! We have another guest!"

We looked at each other curiously while Tante Janna rose to fetch the plate and silverware. Dieter, both curious and too impatient to sit, slipped off his chair and peeked through the parlor archways to the hall. "Papa!" he shrieked and darted around the corner. Katrina's face flushed with happiness as she rose and followed him.

The rest of us left our seats too and clustered around Nils in the hall. He towered over the rest of us. With Dieter perched on one arm and Katrina nestled in the other, looking up at him so pleased, Nils grinned wide enough for the whole world.

Dessert was delayed while Tante Janna served Nils a hot meal. Dieter had begged his Papa to sit beside him. Katrina sat on his other side, and everybody's seats were mixed up. Somehow I was left without a chair.

"There is another chair in the kitchen," Tante Janna told me, not wanting to miss a moment of her daughter's joy.

I started to pull one in, but I stopped near the door, listening. Papa was asking about Cloquet. A fear gnawed inside me. I changed my mind and slipped off to start in on the dishes, working so furiously that I couldn't think of anything else. There were more dishes than I would use in two months, I decided.

I felt lonely, separated from the merry group by a notion of pending disaster. *What did Papa have in mind, asking Nils about Cloquet?* As I dried the dishes, I tried to concentrate on something else, on the Christmas gifts. Nils had brought gifts in a bundle. I wondered if there would be one for me.

I wondered what Papa would give me—had he brought anything? I had told Papa that I was making presents for everyone. Mamma had always done that, and Papa and I had always made something special for her. *Had Papa remembered?* I had not seen him work on anything except those mysterious canvas trousers and flannel shirts. I hoped he wouldn't give me a red union suit, though it would have made a good laugh.

I finished up just after Tante Janna had lit all the candles on the Christmas tree in the parlor. I stood in the archway and watched, entranced, as the candlelight flickered and glistened on the crystal bells. We sang a Christmas carol, and Onkel Peter read the story from the Gospel of Luke. As I listened, I wondered how angels looked, how they sounded. Dieter had told me about his guardian angel. I wondered if I had one. *Probably not—I would be too old.*

I thought of all the other Christmases when worries had never crossed my mind. The pain of missing Mamma rushed into my soul. I was unaware when Onkel Peter started praying. Papa, dear Papa, came over and squeezed my arm and smiled at me. I was glad that everyone else had heads bowed and did not see the two large teardrops fall into my lap.

Onkel Peter appointed Dieter to pass out the gifts. He chose all the gifts wrapped in Tante Janna's fancy white tissue paper first. Since he could not read the labels, he relied on Kirsten to name the person to whom each present belonged. I watched and smiled, all the time worrying whether the gifts I had made would be brushed aside.

Katrina, who looked every bit the young version of Tante Janna, carefully unwrapped her first gift—a sheer silk scarf with a fine silver brooch. Kirsten ripped open hers and cooed with delight over a porcelain nativity set. Onkel Peter teased Dieter by prolonging the unwrapping of his gift with countless questions about what it might be. He finally held up a new silver pocket watch and chain, which he proudly showed off.

Kelda undid the wrapping on her two small gifts with a meticulous delicacy. She smiled with pleasure over the dainty china dishes for her dresser—one with a flowered lid and one with a velvet cushion. Tante Janna undid the knot in the little velvet bag that Dieter brought her and promptly burst into tears of happiness over the pearl necklace from Onkel Peter.

Papa opened his box—a pair of leather slippers. "Now, Janna," he protested. "You spoil me. You think you have to take care of me all the way down to my toes."

"*Ja*, hush," Tante Janna chuckled. "You know it is Christmas." But she herself protested at Onkel Peter's extravagance when she unwrapped a second present from him—a silver tea set with its gleaming pot and tray and matching sugar bowl and creamer.

My hands fluttered with excitement as I untied the yarn on the large square box Dieter brought me. I peeked under the lid. "Oh, Tante Janna! It's too much!" I lifted out a small brown felt hat. Plum-colored velvet lined the wide brim, and a matching silk flower was tucked into the satin band. "I couldn't have imagined anything so fine! But it really is too much," I confessed, concerned.

"Tch! Never mind. It is from both your Papa and us," Tante Janna assured me.

I slipped out of my chair to try on the hat in front of the hall mirror. The brim framed most of my face; the wisps of bangs curled prettily around the edges. I sighed with delight. "It is so beautiful. I hardly know what to say. It's just the hat to go with that plum-colored wool, Papa. Tante Janna, Uncle Peter, Papa—thank you!"

Dieter opened several gifts in a row: a tiny train set, a little engineer's suit, and a wooden whistle that sounded exactly like a train whistle. He grew so excited with the toys that Tante Janna had to remind him that there were still other gifts underneath the tree. He promptly found another gift for himself. I didn't expect his whoop for joy over the sweater set.

"Now I can play outside *twice* every day, Mamma," he told Katrina with a wheedling smile. "I won't have to stay inside because my clothes are wet." He looked longingly out the window at the soft, wet snow falling in thick flakes. "Can I go out now and try them?"

Katrina sighed patiently, but Nils laughed aloud. "Tomorrow I will go outside with you, and we will build a big snowman."

"As tall as you, Papa?"

"Taller. As tall as I can reach."

Dieter's eyes shone with admiration, and Nils grinned with enjoyment.

"*Ja*, we will have a fun day. But you have presents to deliver. What is in those big packages, Dieter?" He pointed to the bundles wrapped in brown paper. Dieter flung his cap and mittens aside and rushed to investigate.

He picked up one and carried it to Kirsten, who had placed her nativity set on an end table and was lovingly arranging the wise men, oblivious to the world. "What does this say, Tante Kirsten?"

Kirsten glanced down at the package. "Papa," she read, turning to adjust the position of a camel. Dieter beamed at his father and headed directly for him. I watched anxiously, knowing he was mistaken, but what could I say? He seemed so delighted that his father had a present.

"Now how did you know that I was coming?" he teased merrily, snapping the string with one pull. Dieter beamed on without answering, but he jumped up and down when Nils held up a sweater that matched Dieter's.

"Papa, we will match just like the twins! Let's go out and play now, Papa!"

Nils laughed. "*Ja*, the thing is—only half of me will fit in this sweater. I do not think the mittens will fit either." He grinned down at Dieter, who looked puzzled. "Do you think maybe this belongs to the Papa of someone else?" he asked gently.

Dieter stood and shook his head.

Nils smiled and winked at him. "Onkel Andrew is Annetti's Papa. What do you think?"

Reluctantly, Dieter took the sweater set and the wrappings and solemnly brought them to Papa, but I saw the tears welling up in his eyes. When Onkel Peter opened his sweater set, Dieter broke into a sob. "You don't have one, Papa! I want you to have one."

"*Ja*, that is all right, Dieter. We can still play outside. Annetti did not know I was coming, so how could she have known to make one just for me?"

"I can start one for your Papa tomorrow, Dieter. Would you like that?"

Dieter quieted and wiped his wet cheeks on his sleeve, but he still looked worried. "Will it be just like mine?"

"Yes," I promised. "Only B - I - G!" I stretched my arms out wide. Nils laughed and protested that he wasn't that big.

Nils had brought presents for Tante Janna's family. The ladies all received small wooden jewelry boxes. Katrina's was made of polished mahogany with a fine gold edging. The others were of cherry. Onkel Peter received a thin wooden case for his surgical instruments, and Dieter received a set of dominoes.

The aprons did not seem so grand after all the other presents, but Tante Janna admired my work. I unwrapped the last gift—one nearly overlooked: a tiny hand-sewn case full of needles. Papa had stitched "proud of you" on the flap. *Dear Papa!* His thoughtfulness brought tears to my eyes. I told him I would cherish it for years to come.

I sat back and watched as Dieter and Kirsten played with their gifts and the older family members visited with each other. Mamma had not been here, but I would always remember this Christmas with a fondness.

I had fond memories of the day that followed as well. I stayed up much of the night knitting that sweater for Nils. Papa let me sleep late during the morning hours, and when we walked to Tante Janna's house for dinner, I discovered that Dieter and Nils had built the biggest family of big snowmen I had ever seen.

Dieter waved to his snow family as we left for the Christmas Day worship service. Gusts of wind swept across and shook the stick arms of the snowmen, making the old mittens wave at us in reply. We all chuckled at the sight.

Lars laughed and laughed when he saw us at church. Dieter and Onkel Peter and Papa all wore their bright red sweaters, caps, scarves, and mittens. Lars had worn his too!

Adelle kept shaking her head over the sight.

"So much knitting—how did you ever finish?" she asked. "The apron you made me is lovely. How can I thank you, Annetti? Inga was delighted with the crib and the little mattress. I wish she could have come to tell you so herself, but she was worried that the little one would catch the croup."

"Is he sick?" I asked, wrinkling my brow with worry.

Adelle laughed and patted my arm. "No, not much. He has the sniffles, but he coos and gurgles when Olin holds him up in the air. He will be fine."

I smiled and relaxed, dropping my arm, but Adelle swept her hand under my elbow and drew me aside from the crowd.

"I must tell you," she added in a hushed tone, her azure eyes piercing mine. "I see you take good care of my Lars. I had worried about him. He looked so thin when he came from the old country, but he looks good now. He cannot say enough about the wonderful meals."

I felt myself blushing and glanced nervously about to see if anyone might have overheard. She was looking across the sanctuary at Lars, so proud and pleased.

Papa winked at me as I turned back toward the crowd. *He couldn't possibly have overhead what was said,* I tried to assure myself. But of course, Papa could imagine. I blushed an even deeper hue and dreaded the teasing that would surely follow.

Lars joined us after the church service for a supper of Tante Janna's leftovers. When he was not commenting on how wonderful the food tasted, he was listening intently to whatever Nils said about Cloquet or asking questions about the town. Papa listened with interest too and asked questions of his own.

My heart sank. *If only his questions hadn't been so practical! Somehow I knew he had plans.*

Then Kelda drew Lars into a long conversation about the wooden jewelry box that Nils had given her, and all the little boxes were brought out for display. I excused myself to help with the dishes. I walked home in the dark, telling Papa that I was tired and wanted to go to bed early.

Sometimes I was so sure Lars liked me. *But "like" is not "love,"* I reminded myself. I feared the attention Lars showed to Kelda. Whenever he was talking to her, he seemed so devoted, so captured by her presence. I couldn't fault him for that. Kelda was beautiful—and wealthy and full of social graces. She'd make a much better match for him than I could ever make. I made myself face that sorrow. Was it lack of faith that made me do so?

Despair filled me. I tried to shake it off by fixing myself a cup of tea. *This Christmas has been a wonderful, special time,* I thought in an effort to cheer myself. *There's the hat and the plum-colored wool waiting to be cut. There is no reason why I should feel so disheartened.*

I thought of Adelle's reminder months before—that to feel her best, a woman needs to take care of herself inside and out. I scolded myself for staying up late. But the lack of sleep had taken its toll: I was emotionally drained.

I tried to assure myself I still had the promise of God's Word that all things work together for good to those who love Him.

I love God, but where is my faith? When Papa talks about Cloquet it doesn't feel as though I have any faith at all. Sleep, blessed sleep—please let me feel better!

11: Growing Pains

I knitted every spare minute of that week, hating the click of my needles. Clo-quet, Clo-quet, Clo-quet, they seemed to repeat. If only Papa and Lars would leave the subject alone! But no! Cloquet became the talk of breakfast, lunch, supper, and evenings. Papa, who was not normally a loquacious or exuberant person, now spoke with an enthusiasm I had never known he possessed.

To him, Cloquet represented a future of hope. A booming lumber town, it offered plenty of work for everyone, even tailors. Most lumberjacks and many of the men at the mills were without wives or families to care for them—or to sew for them, and due to that fact, warm clothing could be sold at a premium during the cold of winter.

Papa had been quietly planning to make use of this opportunity. He had spent the last few months making trousers and flannel shirts and red union suits to send back with Nils, but the more he talked about Cloquet, the more he dreamed of traveling there himself. He began to talk of spending a few weeks there so that he could see the market firsthand. Lars wanted to go too, and they decided to rent a room together.

I listened and bit my tongue. *And then what?* I wanted to ask of their plans. I wanted life to remain as it was, but already my life was changing. Papa himself seemed a different person. I loved him, but I could not bring myself to share his enthusiasm. Seeing his excitement brought a jolt to my very being.

I had lived with Papa for sixteen years (my September birthday had passed unnoticed) and had never seen him act this way. Did I really know him? Had he been this excited when he and Mamma left the old country? I wondered if Mamma had shared his excitement, if she had felt confidence in Papa's plans. Had she possessed the faith that all things would work together for good, as Lars frequently reminded me these days? My faith was undoubtedly small. My mind was filled with doubts.

Papa made his decision without a word of discussion with me. He and Lars left with Nils on New Year's Day. I was to stay indefinitely with Tante Janna and Onkel Peter. I pleaded with Papa over that issue.

I begged him to let me stay by myself and keep the shop open. He would hear none of it. Tante Janna and Onkel Peter would take good care of me, and I was to do everything I could to help them and not become a burden. I did not want to be taken care of, I insisted. I wanted to keep my customers. Papa was silent, refusing to discuss the matter.

I even begged him to take me with him. I could cook for him, I argued. I could keep house and help him fill his orders. I could cook for others as well as for Lars and make a little more money. Papa would not consider any of my ideas. This visit was only for a few weeks, he countered. He and Lars could live more cheaply without me, and Cloquet was not the place for a young, unmarried woman—not with all the lumberjacks and mill boys. Living there had been hard enough on Katrina.

I tried to tell Papa that I was not like Katrina, raised in the lap of luxury. I was like Mamma—used to hard work. When he and Mamma had come here from the old country, hadn't Mamma been a help rather than a burden? But none of my arguments moved him. He left with Lars, taking with him his sewing machine and the remaining bolts of winter fabrics.

The day he left, I moved in a daze. I couldn't talk. I couldn't smile. I followed Tante Janna's family to the docks, as Papa was to sail with Nils to Duluth, where they would catch the train to Cloquet. I stood off to the side and watched as Nils threw Dieter over his shoulder and pretended he was a sack of potatoes to be tossed onto the pile of luggage.

I listened to Dieter's laughter, to Kirsten's unending stream of questions, to the soft inaudible words exchanged between Kelda and Lars. I watched their handshake and lingering gaze. I watched Nils and Katrina embrace. I felt no part of this festive farewell.

Papa came up and put his hands on my shoulders. His eyes bored into mine. "Annetti, you do not have to take it so hard. It is not the end of the world, you know."

I looked at him, not speaking. *No, it is not the end of your world, but it is the end of mine.* Papa would not understand that because he was too excited about the trip. It was the beginning of a new era for him. *I should be happy for him,* I told myself. I managed a weak smile.

"That is better. I will write. I will be home before you know it." He smiled and gave me a long look. I fought to keep back the tears. Then he was gone.

Life seemed unbearable after that. I was put in Kelda's room, a situation she clearly disdained. I had always admired Kelda's easy manner and social graces, but now I saw a different side of her, an arrogance and meanness that pained me to no end.

Often, when I entered the room, she would sniff, shake her blond curls, and leave. When Tante Janna was present, she acted civil enough, but when we had cause to be alone, she would mutter about the lack of space. Under her breath, she would deplore the necessity of aiding cousins who lived in penury and were likely to sponge off their better-off relations indefinitely. She made me feel quite beneath her dignity.

I did not like the situation either. I had also been accustomed to having my own room. But I felt at fault, and I did everything I could to give her more space and privacy. I slept on the very edge of the double bed to avoid crowding her. I took to rising early, quietly washing, dressing, and fetching fresh water, warmed just for her use. I stayed up late, under the guise of working on my plum-colored suit, so that she would be asleep when I crawled into bed.

Somehow, despite the largeness of her room, I never felt there was space for me. She had a fine wardrobe for her clothes instead of hooks, but her wardrobe was full. Every drawer in the bureau was stuffed. I didn't know what to do with the few clothes I had brought. When I folded them and hung them over the upholstered chair, she made faces and complained of having nowhere to sit. I finally decided to slide them under the bed.

Since Papa had not wanted me to be a burden, I helped wherever I could. I washed dishes, scrubbed floors, and entertained Dieter. I emptied chamber pots and scoured them every morning. I stood over laundry tubs and before the ironing board for hours. I was sent to fetch coal from the cellar and wood for the kitchen stove. When it snowed, I swept off the front and back porches and shoveled a path to the carriage house and privy. I allowed myself no time, no rest from the strain.

Three weeks passed. I was standing at the kitchen table grinding chunks of beef, pork, and veal for Tante Janna's meatballs when Onkel Peter came in with several letters. He was still in his overcoat and fur hat. "One for you," he announced, handing Tante Janna an envelope. She took it and glanced at the handwriting. "And one for Katrina and one for Kelda," he stated, grinning with delight. He had reached inside his coat and slipped the envelopes from his shirt pocket, holding them out for her to inspect.

Tante Janna looked up, her eyebrows arched in surprise. "This one is from Andrew," she stated and glanced at the others. "They are all from Cloquet, only one is not the handwriting of Nils or Andrew."

"The letter for Kelda," Onkel Peter remarked with a wink. He removed his coat and hung it on a hook by the back door to the clinic. Another letter peeked out from his shirt pocket. Whose letter was that?

Tante Janna's face broke into a grin. "*Ja, ja.* She will be happy. She is in the dining room with Dieter, playing dominoes." Onkel Peter winked at her again and was gone.

My hopes fell. Surely Papa would have written to me as well as to Tante Janna. *But Onkel Peter would have given me the letter if it were mine,* I reasoned silently. I continued grinding meat. Tante Janna put a teakettle on the stove and sat down at the table across from me. She slipped a hairpin from the generous rolls of sandy hair and slit her envelope. As she read, I watched with interest the emotions that danced across her face.

Onkel Peter returned to present an envelope to me. "Last but not least," he announced with a flourish. *Strange that he should use those words. I do feel "least."* My hands were too greasy to take the letter. I looked at it longingly.

"Put it on the sideboard," Tante Janna directed before I could reply. She glanced up only momentarily. "Her hands are full of vurk. She can read it when she is done with the meat." She sighed. "Such a girl for vurk! She has more done in three weeks than I think to do in a month'." She shuffled the pages of Papa's letter, and out fell a five-dollar bill.

"*Uff da!* That I did not expect. He must be doing well." She read on silently, then wrinkled her brow and folded the letter.

"Is everything fine?" Onkel Peter asked, joining Tante Janna at the table for a cup of tea.

"*Ja, ja,*" she answered slowly. "He has sold all the clothes he took with him *and,*" she emphasized that word, looking significantly at Onkel Peter, "he is staying on for a while to make more. Business is booming." The cold, businesslike tone of her last line did not escape me. She slipped the five-dollar bill into her apron pocket and handed Onkel Peter the letter. "Here, you may read it if you like."

Onkel Peter glanced over the letter and raised his eyebrows over one part, but he didn't say anything. He simply shook his head and slipped the letter back into his pocket. Something about the way his silver curls moved reminded me of Kelda. I felt disdain I'd never felt from him before. Was I trapped in a houseful of people who seemed to shun or ignore my presence?

The teakettle rattled on the stove. "Tea is ready," Tante Janna stated. "I was going to take some to Katrina. She is not feeling well. Perhaps you should look in on her, Peter." She cast a meaningful look at him while she fixed a tray.

I finally finished my work and covered the bowl of ground meat with a clean cloth. Tante Janna was particular about how many times meat for her meatballs had to be put through the grinder with spices. Three times for each meat, she insisted—veal, pork, and beef. With the letter business, I had lost count. I had probably ground it ten times. Such grinding, I had learned, was one secret to the making of her famous meatballs.

I had been hoping Tante Janna would let me have her recipe. I had watched her make the meatballs before, trying to memorize the ingredients—finely chopped onion, grated potatoes, allspice, pepper, milk, and egg. But she seemed particular about exactly how much of each and not very willing to explain. I sighed. A lesson in her culinary marvels would have to wait for another day.

I washed my hands in a basin of water, scrubbing them with soft brown soap. Then I dried them on my apron, took my letter off the sideboard, and slipped into the pantry, closing the door behind me. Privacy was a welcome reprieve.

Large crocks lined the sides of the long pantry. Above them stretched shelves filled with jars. *Tante Janna's pantry smells like the general store*, I thought, as I pulled a stool out from under the pastry table. A tall window above it provided plenty of light.

I sat down and opened the envelope, pulling out several folded sheets. Papa had written in Norwegian. I could almost hear his voice speaking the words as I read.

Dear Annetti,

The trip to Duluth was long and cold. I was glad for the sweater, hat, and scarf that you made. Mittens and socks too. Lars and Nils also. We had to stay two nights in Duluth. The trains could not go through. Ten- and twelve-foot snow over the tracks. Took two days to clear. Nils was worried about his work. "Not to worry," Lars says. "All things work together for good. See? Annetti's knitting worked together for good. We are warm."

Duluth sits on steep hills. Cloquet has steep hills too, but we are renting a room near the flat of the river valley. The railroad is nearby. Mills too. Always much noise. The house is kept by Mrs. Higdon. She is a good woman if one does not count cooking or cleaning. Both of us miss your meals and endless washing.

I have sold all the clothes I brought. I will stay to make more, as there is much need. I do not know how long. I sent money to your Tante Janna for your needs. She is a kind woman to take care of you. Be patient and work hard to help her. Remember: all things work together for good, to those who love God. I trust you do and will.

Tears came to my eyes. They blurred the last line so that I had to blink and strain to make out the words. "With much love, Your Papa," he had written. I should have been happy.

"*Ja*, much love," I thought, pronouncing the words to myself in Papa's accent. *Why does love have to hurt?* So I would have to stay here longer, while Tante Janna and Onkel Peter make faces and Kelda exudes cool contempt.

First I lose Mamma, I pouted, *and then Papa—and with him everything I hold dear. Everything except work.* "Vurk"—that was always Papa's cure. I was to work hard, only I was so tired of working endlessly with no relief, no reward in sight. I put my head down on my arms and closed my eyes in despair. There was nothing I could do about it, either. *Nothing.* And I was tired...so tired.

12: Testing the Promise

I awoke to the sound of Kelda's voice coming from the kitchen. "I do not wish to be imposed upon. It was rude of him to expect us to keep her so that he can go off however long he wants."

"*Ja,* but he is family, Kelda. I was glad to help him when he needs. It vurks both ways. Annetti has been a wonderful help to me these last three weeks with housework and with Dieter."

There was a silence. I could imagine Kelda's taciturn frown as she shook her blond curls. Then she cut my heart to the quick: "I do not wish to continue sharing my room with the maid."

"For shame, Kelda! She is your cousin, not a maid, despite her willingness to help. I think I have taught you to be gracious, and then I hear such talk. What have I taught you?"

Kelda sighed and recited the answer. "The ability to be gracious in all circumstances is the mark of a fine lady, a skill only achieved through constant self-control of emotions and desires."

"Very good. And now, I remember that you were complaining about no-t'ing decent to wear. Perhaps while Annetti is here, she can make you a new dress or perhaps one of those new suits?" There was a pause.

"Five dollars—for me, Mamma?"

"For the fabric. Think about what you want."

I held my breath. Footsteps. Then quiet. A flood of emotions filled me. Anger raged—anger at Papa for making me stay here, at Kelda for degrading Papa, at Tante Janna for giving to Kelda the money that Papa had sent for my needs.

Sorrow overwhelmed me—grief over Kelda's unwillingness to consider me a friend. Even Tante Janna seemed to measure my worth in the volume of my work, not in the pleasure of my company. I felt desolate, without anyone who truly cared for me.

Well! I would have to pay attention and learn on my own. I would strive for the inner beauty Lars had talked about one evening, the fruits of the Spirit: love, joy, peace, longsuffering, gentleness, goodness, faithfulness, meekness, and self-control.

An ache grew in my heart. I missed those conversations with Lars. I desperately wished he had written to me instead of to Kelda. *Oh, how hard it is not to want for oneself the pleasures others so obviously enjoy! If only I could simply accept my humble position as a servant!*

Resolve grew in my heart and mind. I would ask God to help me change. I would control my anger and selfishness; I would be helpful, gracious, and cheerful for however long I stayed.

Not long after, Onkel Peter suggested cleaning out the attic and moving in furniture from my room above the shop. I wondered if Kelda, with her schemes, had suggested as much. I felt uneasy about the idea of sleeping in the attic so isolated from everyone else, but I kept silent. At last I was to have my own room.

I had never seen Tante Janna's attic. I should have realized that like her house, it too was grand, even if the walls were unfinished and the rafters bare. Tante Janna paid someone to move Papa's parlor stove from the shop to the attic, where it was piped into the chimney.

After the attic was warm, I started scrubbing with pails of steaming water and Tante Janna's fragrant pine solution. It took me two whole days. By that time I had been charmed by the views the attic windows offered.

The attic stairwell was wrapped inside the south gable, and two wide windows lit the landing where the stairs turned. The windows overlooked the roof to the clinic, but the sun streamed through them gloriously. There was a door at the bottom flight, but none at the top—only a railing around the edges. I felt as if I were walking up the steps to a castle turret.

The windows at the north gable brought views of Lake Superior I had never known existed. I would tuck my bed into this gable, I resolved, and watch the boats creeping over the waves. On warmer days, when I could slide up the window sash to shake out the dust mop, I would stick my head out and look across to the housetops of Washburn and the woods of Bayfield Ridge.

Onkel Peter paid two men to move the furniture. I felt satisfied that I'd received at least some benefit from the five dollars Papa had sent for my care. My small mirror was hung above the washstand next to the bed, and the board with a row of hooks for my clothes was mounted on the wall opposite.

When I had hung the curtains, made up the bed with my quilt, and put my braided rag rug before the washstand, I felt more at home than I had in weeks.

I would never have asked for more, but then Kelda stood at the top of the stairs and surveyed the rest of the attic.

"We could do a great deal more if *Mor* would let us." Her blue eyes fairly sparkled with mischief.

"What do you mean?"

"It's so empty. Look at those windows." She pointed to the front gable. "They look so bare. They need some lace curtains, and a couple of chairs with a little table in between."

My heart gave a grateful jump. Mamma's furniture from the shop parlor! How I would love to have it nearby. "And the carpet," I added eagerly. "The Persian carpet with a fringe. Do you think Tante Janna would allow it?"

Kelda raised her eyebrows and looked at me slyly. "Those chairs will rot without a regular cleaning. The carpet too. Your mother's probably turning in her grave right now over the fact that they haven't been brushed or swept for more than a month. Besides, you'll need her machine and a table and chair for your sewing."

I grinned with happiness. For once I was glad that Kelda knew how to get her way. She wheedled her parents into having the men move nearly all of our remaining furniture. She may have been decorating a play house, but it was to be my play house.

I hauled the smaller stuff on my old sled, and together we hung the lace curtains and fixed up a small sitting room in the west gable beside the stairwell. Complete with the basket of magazines and a lamp, it was a cozy spot to relax, right next to the warmth of the little stove. It proved a pleasant place to visit evenings, when the sun warmed the room.

Before the large windows at the back gable of the house, we put the kitchen table with its three chairs, along with Mamma's sewing machine. It was a perfect place to work in the morning, for the windows faced east, providing bright light until noon.

The sideboard fit neatly against the angled wall between the stairwell and the east gable. Along the wall between the table and my bed, I stood Mamma's dressmaking form. I tucked her trunk and the dressy fabrics Papa had left into a nook between the gables.

After we finished arranging my treasures, we sat in Mamma's chairs and sighed with satisfaction. I had to admit that Kelda had done a wonderful job at decorating. I was delighted to feel surrounded by home.

Not much remained in the shop or our living quarters above: Only Papa's bedstead, the wood stove in the kitchen, and the shop counter. I had given everything a thorough cleaning and locked the doors, wondering when and if I would return.

At last, life settled into a peaceful, even happy routine. I slept better. I spent most of my mornings working on the dark blue linen skirt and jacket that Kelda had chosen. We grew to be friends and cousins again over that suit and its striped silk shirtwaist.

Sometimes Kelda would bring Dieter, and while he played with his wooden train and little clothespin men, we would talk. We would make tea for ourselves on the little parlor stove and serve it in Mamma's few pieces of china. Kelda would try on whatever I had finished, admiring herself in Mamma's oval mirror, which we had finally decided to hang in stairwell where the steps turned. Kelda would pour over all the issues of *Godey's Lady's Book*, laughing over some of the fashions and chattering endlessly over others.

Sometimes Kirsten would come too, and we'd fuss over how to fix her long, straight hair for the day. I had figured out how to make bows from the leftover fancy fabrics in Mamma's sewing basket, and Kirsten's supply of those steadily grew along with her dislike of hairbrushes.

Katrina always read to Dieter in the late morning, while I was helping with dinner. After dinner and dishes, I would take my turn at entertaining the boy. We would bundle up and head outside for a hike, carrying a basket packed with gingersnaps or molasses cookies or whatever Tante Janna had me bake for the week. Dieter would hunt for deer tracks and play Indian scout. We'd make snow angels and paths for playing "fox and goose." Sometimes we'd slide back and forth on one of the ponds or build snow houses overlooking the bay. On warmer days, we'd stay out until the sun started to set. Then we'd come in wet and tired and hungry for supper.

"Thank you, Annetti," Tante Janna would say as we tramped to the cellar to hang up our wet garments. "I am glad you can keep up with him. Now, let's see how strong you are, Dieter."

"I'm strong like Papa, *Bestemor*—look," Dieter would jump up on top of the ice chest and hang onto one of the clotheslines. "I'm hanging from a tree branch. Can you do this?"

"*Ja*, sure," she would laugh, reaching up for a clothesline. "And when you grow as strong as *Bestemor*, you can pull yourself up all the way to the chin." She would pull on the clothesline until it came to a point just below her chin.

Dieter would cock his head sideways and grin. "You're too tall to do it right, *Bestemor*. Let me show you." He would try and try, swinging back and forth and making the clothes bounce up and down, but he never could touch his chin to the clothesline.

Tante Janna would laugh and shake her head. "The exercise is good for the boy," she'd tell me. "He sleeps better."

After supper and dishes, Katrina would give Dieter a good washing and tuck him into bed. The rest of us would sit in the parlor and chuckle over his complaints. He always had a new reason why he shouldn't be scrubbed.

Then everyone would talk. Onkel Peter would amuse us with stories of his patients' idiosyncrasies, and Kelda would elaborate on the gossip of the women callers they had received that afternoon. I had to smile to myself when I watched her. She would talk and talk and crochet a few loops, then have to stop and count again and check her pattern. She did more counting than a pupil in a primer.

I listened as I worked on my wool quilt. I was making it out of small squares individually stuffed, which I would later sew together. It would be a wonderfully warm quilt when I finished. I was making it big enough for Papa's bedstead. It seemed there was no end to the little squares needing to be stuffed and sewn.

Later I would go up to my attic room to work on my plum-colored suit or copy recipes or write Papa a letter. I wrote many more letters than I received, much longer ones too. I filled them with the details of my day—the views from my windows, the antics of Dieter, our afternoon adventures, Onkel Peter's remedies.

When Papa's letters became fewer, I wrote to ask him questions about Cloquet, but his response was brief: "Cloquet is the same as Nils said—plenty of vurk. When you come, you will see. But we will build a house first."

I sighed and bit my lip. I had known this decision would come. I had stopped fighting against fate. My future hung on his promise that I would follow him to Cloquet, on God's promise that all things would work out for good. I wondered when the time would come, or if it would indeed come at all.

Chapter 13: Heartache

The bitterly cold weeks of winter passed, slowly melting into spring. I finished the outfit for Kelda as well as ones for other family members. Tante Janna had me sewing for Kirsten, Katrina, and Dieter too, and even a suit for herself.

During those cold winter months, the bolts of Mamma's dress fabrics—the lighter-colored wools, silks, or velvets that Papa had not deigned to take—dwindled from the stash in the nook near my table. They never asked to purchase Mamma's fabrics. They just chose and ordered, apparently considering it my duty to donate Mamma's fabrics as well as my time.

The assumption grated on my sense of justice, but I tried to ignore it, especially after Papa's instructions not to be a burden. I knew I was already costing Tante Janna money for food as well as coal. The sacks of coal from our cellar had been used up for some time. I made myself work longer and harder to make up for the loss.

As the bolts disappeared, my concern for my own wardrobe heightened. I had finished my plum-colored wool suit, but I had concealed it in Mamma's trunk along with the hat, for I didn't have a shirtwaist fit to match. I dared not use the bolt of cream-colored silk that I'd hidden under my mattress late one evening. Kelda had admired it that afternoon, and I had panicked. I hadn't wanted the Nelsons to consume that bolt too, and I nervously tried to divert any conversation that would prompt Kelda's memory of it. I had plans for that bolt.

Oh, how I wished that I had listened to Papa and started more suits for myself! My dresses began to look so shabby next to Kelda's new ones, but no one else seemed to care.

Inwardly, I sighed and tried to be patient, waiting for all things to work together for good—for me, because I loved God. "When Papa returns to get me—" I'd think, and then, remembering Papa's recent letter, my hope would die. Papa had bought a piece of property in Cloquet, on the hill of Carlton Avenue not far from the house Nils was building for Katrina. Papa had promised to send for me when the new shop was built, but that would be months away. How I missed him!

Tante Janna started me on a new spring dress for Kirsten. Kirsten had been allowed to choose the fabric from the general store, a cream-colored polished cotton with pale pink roses. I spent hours tatting the intricate collar and cuffs.

Then Katrina wanted more new clothes for Dieter—velvet knickers with matching suspenders. I cut and stitched and sewed, and Dieter wore them like a prince. He behaved so regally that Katrina began calling him her little gentleman. He would strut down the aisle at church, pausing to inspect the churchgoers with a sedate benevolence. One Sunday he nearly had the whole congregation chuckling.

"God is good," he announced with a satisfied smile.

"*Ja*, that is so," someone would respond.

"He is making us a new baby. I am going to be a big brother. My mamma told me so."

Ladies would blush and titter at the news. I nearly choked, wondering why I had not guessed the fact sooner. How was it that I could live in the same house and be so blind and deaf to its secrets? So many details now made sense—Katrina's late mornings in bed because she did not feel well, the afternoon naps, the new wardrobe she was considering. I shook my head. More sewing!

My work was like slave labor, I complained to myself. But life was no different for most children. I knew most parents regularly collected their children's earnings until they reached full adulthood, age twenty-one. Some parents doled a small portion back to the child for spending money. Papa had been quite generous with me, despite his frugality otherwise. He had let me keep my earnings.

Only now I had none. How ironic that in the midst of the Nelsons' obvious affluence, they couldn't part with any allowance for me! The incident with Dieter seemed to underscore my inferior standing; I had to learn about Katrina's pregnancy many weeks after the rest of the family had known.

I couldn't harbor hard feelings against Dieter. The slight was none of his doing, and I couldn't spoil his joy. I smiled and told him, "You are a little gentleman, and you will be a wonderful big brother, I am sure."

Dieter's eyes brightened. "Gentlemen have horses and fine carriages, and they take pretty ladies out for rides."

"Dieter, you are only a little gentleman—too little to own horses," I reminded him fondly.

"I want to drive *Bestefar's* horses. Can I?"

"You'll have to ask him, Dieter. They are his horses."

Onkel Peter looked thoughtful when Dieter asked him later. "I was going to read my latest medical journal this afternoon, Dieter. Maybe Kelda can take you out with the surrey and horses. Some other day I'll teach you how to hitch up the surrey."

I stood in awe of Kelda's easy manner with horses. Papa had never owned animals, and consequently, I had never learned to feel comfortable with the creatures. Not so with Kelda! Onkel Peter had always kept a pair of sleek brown Trotters to pull his surrey or sleigh. Though he kept a clinic in Ashland, he traveled surrounding areas as well. Despite her prissy manner in other areas, Kelda had always adored the horses. She had often accompanied Onkel Peter on his rounds, begging to drive the horses just as Dieter was now.

So began the drives that tortured my soul. At least once a week, Kelda and Dieter drove out to Olin Sorenson's farm. She would visit with Adelle and Inga, sharing her latest letter from Lars and swapping recipes. Later she would climb to my attic workroom to check on the progress of her next outfit. She would chat while I worked. Our friendship, I realized sadly, had grown rather one-sided: I existed only to listen and exclaim over her good fortune.

Nonetheless, my soul clung to the news about Lars. My heart yearned for more, even though each tidbit pierced me with pain and longing. Lars had not written to me. I had grown so fond of him and of Adelle, but now there seemed no room for me in their lives.

Sometimes Kelda sat all afternoon at the table, writing to Lars in her flowery script while I sewed. Often it would be my task to deliver her letters to the post office along with Tante Janna's correspondence. Oh, how my heart ached!

I cried out to God in my misery, for I had no other outlet. I couldn't reveal my true feelings to Kelda or Tante Janna: I feared their contempt. I wished Mamma was still here. I needed her more than ever now. I couldn't tell Papa. I wrote him long, descriptive letters full of cheerful news, trying to hide my growing agony.

I remembered how Lars talked to God. At night, I would weep silently into my pillow, whispering my sorrows to God, asking for help. Things Lars had told me came to mind. Jesus would understand. He too was rejected and despised, a servant of low esteem. He was a friend to the fatherless, to all those oppressed. I found comfort in reading through the Psalms.

When April arrived, I began spending more time outside—both in Tante Janna's garden and Mamma's flower garden behind the shop. I would work for hours turning over the moist dirt with a shovel and hoeing and raking the clods into even ground.

Then I would clean up at the pump and go inside the shop. I kept the key in my coat pocket, for the weather was still chilly enough to warrant wraps. I swept and scrubbed the bare rooms again, while memories bombarded me. Papa intended to sell the shop with the apartment above. It needed to be ready.

One day, I was standing outside the shop, locking the front shop door, when I spotted a stranger's reflection in the dark, empty shop window. Startled, I turned to find a trim young gentleman dressed in a fine black overcoat and top hat. He smiled and bowed with a flourish. His leather-gloved hand held his snowy white muffler in place as he moved.

Shy but flushed with sudden pleasure, I nodded briefly.

"Your shop is empty," he stated.

I hesitated. "Yes. Papa will be selling it, as we're moving to Cloquet." I swallowed hard over those last words.

"How fortuitous! I would be interested in buying it. Allow me to introduce myself. Allen Hollings, Esquire. And you are?"

"Annetti Sorenson."

"*Miss* Annetti Sorenson?"

I nodded again and flushed as he held out his gloved hand. I looked up into his dark, handsome face—only for a moment. My emotions caught me off guard. I extended my bare, work-worn hand, and he grasped it warmly, sending a thrill up my arm.

Is this the feeling that Kelda called "waking up"?

"My pleasure, Miss Sorenson. I would be so grateful if you would communicate my interest to your father and see that he is presented with my card." He held out a small white card.

Just as I reached for it, I heard Onkel Peter's gig and Dieter's voice calling out for me to watch him drive the horses. Kelda leaned down to speak to Dieter. The gig stopped before us.

"Good afternoon," Mr. Hollings called up to her, tipping his hat politely.

"To you too," called down Kelda. I felt an odd stab of the old jealousy at her lingering gaze. A coy smile formed on her lips, and she tore her eyes from the stranger to look at me in an almost accusing fashion.

"Mr. Hollings, I'd like you to meet my cousin, Miss Kelda Nelson," I announced. "Kelda, this is Mr. Allen Hollings, Esquire. He is interested in buying Papa's shop." I turned to Mr. Hollings, only to find him captivated by Kelda's beauty.

She formed a picture of delight. Her bright blond curls streamed from her stylish blue hat and cascaded down the brilliant blue of her wool coat. Mamma had made the coat for her last winter, spending hours on the fashionable tucks at the waist and the double row of brass buttons.

Mamma had made me a coat like Kelda's in forest green, but I had worn my old, brown coat for working in the garden. I felt shabby, but I swallowed and went on. "Kelda Nelson is the daughter of Dr. Peter Nelson, and Dieter here is her nephew."

"Miss Nelson," the stranger repeated with another flourish and a bow. He tipped his hat to Dieter, calling him "Master Dieter." Dieter crowed with delight.

"My pleasure," Kelda replied with a charming smile. "But you must pardon our short acquaintance. Dieter needs a frolic in the country more than these horses do, I fear. Come and join us, Annetti."

Without ado, I pocketed the card and key, circled around the back of the gig, and climbed up next to Dieter. I didn't relish the thought of how plain and drab I looked beside Kelda. *But no matter,* I thought, *Mr. Hollings won't notice; he's too busy staring at Kelda.*

While we drove, Kelda quizzed me on my meeting with the handsome stranger. She seemed reluctant to believe that we had just exchanged introductions ourselves and that I had not extracted any more information from him than she gained from the introduction. When I showed her the card, she examined it closely and then changed the subject, reminding Dieter to turn right.

I looked around, startled. We were turning into the long driveway before Olin's white farmhouse. A big, black dog, barking wildly but wagging his tail furiously, ran up alongside us. Dieter grinned with pleasure and drove the horses around the loop of the driveway in the back yard. "You have company!" he announced merrily at the top of his lungs, while Kelda tried to shush him.

"*Ja,* I see," remarked Olin, emerging from the tool shed behind us.

I swallowed hard. His voice sounded so much like Lars' jovial responses. His square jaw and ready grin, his shock of wavy golden hair, his moustache—I felt pangs of disappointment and at the same time fear.

What was I doing here? What would I say?

"Inga and Adelle would love to see you," he assured us, as he tied the reins to the hitching post. "Go on inside."

I hung behind the others. The aroma of freshly baked bread greeted us at the door. Adelle hurried from the kitchen, wiping her hands on her apron. The sandy braids circling her head looked more silver than I had remembered. Her face brightened even more when her azure eyes fell on Dieter.

"Are you cold?" she asked. "Would you like some warm milk?"

"No, but I'm hungry," Dieter offered. "I could eat a cookie—more than one."

"Dieter—" Kelda began to admonish.

Adelle waved her off with an easy chuckle. "Now I think I should know that. I have never met a boy who was not hungry. Come. Sit down. I find something here for you. Fresh bread and butter?"

Dieter nodded. He had finished two thick slices by the time Inga came down with the baby, now a large, wiggling ball of smiles and coos. Dieter wiped his hands on the seat of his knickers and raced to the parlor to watch the baby hitch himself around on the large rag rug. Kelda, comfortable with weeks of previous visits, followed him, conversing freely with Inga.

I found a pan of water and a pile of potatoes and carrots at the end of the table. As usual, I made myself useful. I peeled quietly, watching the fuss Adelle made over Dieter, wondering if she had treated Lars the same way when he was little. After Dieter and Kelda had exited to the parlor, she turned to me. I felt compassion pouring from her eyes.

"Annetti, you always vurk, *ja?*"

I shrugged and smiled briefly at her while she studied me. "Papa was always happy to have me work. My ability to work seems to be what people appreciate most about me."

Adelle looked at me for a long moment. "You are worth far more than your vurk," she said soberly. "I wish more people would realize that. You look thin and worn out. How do you do without your Papa?"

I shrugged again. "I have what I need at Tante Janna's."

"You have a letter from him, *ja*?"

I nodded and forced myself to say the words. "I have instructions to ask Onkel Peter's help in selling the shop. Papa is building a small one in Cloquet. I am to move there when it's done, but that may be months away."

"Ah, you are young and strong. You will be a big help to him." Adelle paused and smiled, her light blue eyes filled with affection.

I stared up at her, clinging to her buoyant confidence. *That's what makes her so attractive,* I realized. *She cares deeply about those around her, and she fills them with cheer and hope. I must work to be like that.*

"I have a letter too. Just this afternoon." She pulled a folded paper from her large apron pocket. "Would you like to read it?"

I started with surprise and then nodded with a shy smile. I set aside the peeling, washed my hands, and sat down to read, trying not to show how eager I felt. The letter was written in an odd square sort of script, the same script that I had seen on the envelopes Kelda received regularly from Cloquet. I swallowed hard and glanced up. Adelle had disappeared. I heard her voice from the parlor, conversing with Kelda and Inga.

I scanned the contents of the letter from Lars. He was working on the pantry shelves of Nils' new house. A crew had finished the tarpaper shell, and now they were nailing on the clapboard siding. Nils had hired Lars to finish the trim—cupboards, mantle, staircase, windows, doors, and baseboards. Others were handling the plaster and tiling the roof.

Lars had found property for a church. The plot stood at the top of the hill. My father had purchased a plot for his shop across the street from the church, and building the shop promised more income for Lars after Nils' job was finished.

"See, Mamma," he wrote in Norwegian. "All things work together for good. I will have my church. Andrew will have his shop, and Nils will have his house." In the recesses of my memory, I could hear his voice saying those words in English with his heavy Norwegian accent.

My eyes burned with tears. *Good for him. Good for Papa, Good for Nils, but what about me?* I no longer existed in Lars' world, and yet I missed him. I missed Papa above all. Quietly, I folded the letter and set it on the table, sucking in my breath, sucking in the pain. My eyes caught the lines written on the back page.

I picked up the letter again. There was a postscript, also in Norwegian: "Mamma, I have thought and prayed about this matter for months. I am going to ask Kelda Nelson to be my wife. I love her. You must know from her visits that she is a fine woman as well as a beauty. I hope that I have your blessing."

I exhaled. Any shred of hope with which Adelle had sought to fill me fled. My shoulders drooped. I looked up to see if anyone had noticed, but Adelle had still not returned.

Surely she had not meant for me to see that note! Had she even known it was there? *"I wish that other people would realize you are worth far more than your work,"* she had told me. *Had she meant Lars? What would she write to him? Which of us would receive her blessing? How could she not give it to Kelda?*

I set the letter on the other end of the table, flipped so that the postscript did not lie in plain sight. Quickly, I busied myself with the last of the peeling. I added the potatoes and carrots to the pot roast simmering on the stove, along with several small onions.

I forced myself to sit down and write out my recipe for brown oatmeal rolls, to leave as a gift for Adelle and Inga. Work—I needed work. I dared not let myself think or feel.

14: The Unexpected

All the next morning, I ironed sheets. I sprinkled them with water until they were damp. Then I folded them in half and fed them over the wooden ironing board, pressing hot irons over one side and then the other until the sheets lay flat and stiff. The smell of clean, hot cotton wafted up from the irons—a smell I found familiar and comforting.

I worked near the wood stove in the kitchen, where I could easily trade off irons, letting the cooled one re-heat on the side burner while I continued ironing with another. I wore a quilted mitt on my right hand, for the wooden handle on the irons was often too hot to grab without one. During the brisk cold of morning, the warmth felt good on my hands.

Around ten o'clock, Tante Janna returned from the post office. Her plump figure entered through the front door. She stopped in her husband's office to drop off his stack of mail, smiled at all my piles of sheets in passing, and then poked her head through the open clinic door. "Kelda, you have a letter. I will set it on the sideboard."

"I'm unpacking the liniment that arrived yesterday," Kelda called back. "I'll be there in a moment."

Tante Janna set the letter on the sideboard and sat down at the table with a sigh. "It is so nice to have your help, Annetti. You do such fine vurk." She set down a package of meat wrapped in white paper, slipped off her shawl, and untied the ribbons on her hat.

I smiled and murmured my thanks, continuing to work.

"I would like you to take care of dinner today," she announced, hanging her hat on a corner of a nearby chair and smoothing her thick hair.

"What should I make?"

"Mock duck and a carrot ring with creamed peas. Rolls, of course. And mincemeat pie for dessert. You will find the recipes in the drawer of the sideboard."

I arched my eyebrows in surprise. "Are we having company?"

She smiled slyly, raising her eyebrows but looking down toward the right until her eyes were slits with dark corners. "Perhaps."

Pleased that she trusted me with such an unusually fancy menu, I quickly finished the last sheet and the pillowcases and scrambled to find the recipes. I couldn't help noticing the letter on the sideboard. "Kelda Nelson, Ashland, Wisconsin" was printed in large, neat letters of that same odd, square-shaped script I knew belonged to Lars. The postmark was from Cloquet. Kelda had let the letter sit. How unusual!

Someone knocked at the front door as I was stuffing the pork tenderloin with apples and boiled prunes. I didn't hear Tante Janna's footsteps on the stairs, so I called for Kelda to answer the front door. She sighed as she brushed past me, looking smart in her navy skirt and blue-and-white striped shirtwaist. It was the stranger, wishing to see me about an offer on the shop.

"My father has been authorized to handle the sale," I heard Kelda announce from the front hall. "He's finishing up with a patient. I'll let him know you are here. You may wait in his office."

I heard her walk through his office and rap on the other door to the clinic, the one that opened into an examining room. There were muffled voices and finally Onkel Peter's warm greeting. I heard him ask Kelda to grab a notebook, and then the door closed.

Inwardly, I fumed. *Why should I be excluded from this meeting—and Kelda attend? It's MY father's shop!* It seemed another injustice added to a long list of wrongs. *Kelda wore the beautiful clothes that I had made from Mamma's fabrics, while my clothes grew drab. Kelda received a generous allowance for her part-time work in the apothecary shop, while I received only empty thanks for my endless hours of labor.* I glanced at the letter on the sideboard. *She had Lars, while I—*

Dissatisfaction filled my soul like poison until I remembered Pastor Lyndahl's last sermon: God orders the affairs of men. Like Job, we must not charge God with wrongdoing but humbly accept the bad as well as the good that He allows to come into our lives. We must trust that God will reward every person justly in the Day of Judgment, that He will execute revenge when it is due. "Let us walk as people of faith," he had urged. I thought of Lars and his stinging words that one Sunday afternoon: "Oh, ye of little faith!"

Oh, God! I cried in a whisper. *You show your love to Kelda. Love me too. Help my unbelief!*

*　　　　　*　　　　　*

Mr. Allen Hollings, Esquire, stayed for dinner, which I served as if I were a maid, only eating afterward. Kelda sat next to him, across the table from the kitchen door. Every time I entered the room, I saw her blue eyes fastened on his. To be fair, everyone's eyes seemed riveted to his. I flitted about the room, filling water glasses and replenishing the basket of cloverleaf rolls.

I went unnoticed while I drank in the details. Looks of cozy camaraderie passed between Kelda and Mr. Hollings. She offered to direct the decoration of the shop and the living quarters above. His gaze lingered on her smile. Their actions reminded me of an earlier dinner, when the dark head had been golden blond. This time I felt no jealousy. I felt numb.

While the others enjoyed their pie and coffee, Dieter and I ate at the pastry table in the pantry, hidden away from the others. He had been playing with the neighbor boy and had come home smeared with mud, unfit for the sight of company. Katrina had cleaned him up and put him in my charge, busy as I was with serving dinner. Today he was full of chatter.

"Mamma said our baby is going to be born in the fall. Papa is building a big house, and I'm going to have my own room! Our baby will have a room too. And we're going to live there before the leaves turn colors." He shoveled two more bites into his mouth. "Where are you going to live?" he asked, with his mouth full.

"My Papa is building a shop up on the hill—across from the Norwegian Lutheran church. I'll live with my Papa above the shop, just like I did here."

"We're going to take a train all the way to Cloquet."

"Really?" I asked. That was news to me. I had heard that the Wisconsin Central Railroad Company was just putting the finishing touches on Ashland's new train station. One could travel to Superior and Duluth or all the way to Madison, Milwaukee, or even Chicago. The improvements boded well for the summer resorts.

"And you're going to come to help."

"I see. Would you like that?"

Dieter smiled and nodded. I smiled back at his innocence, but it grated on my nerves that all these plans were made without the least bit of consideration to me. I was the last one to know anything.

I wondered what other decisions I was missing. I spent the rest of the day preaching Pastor Lyndahl's sermon to myself over and over again.

*   *   *

Kelda moved in a continual flutter of excitement over decorating the shop. Allen—as she freely called him now—was going to establish a law office. He had contracted a work crew to transform the shop. Within days, the bare rooms were buzzing with men sanding the floors and plastering the walls. The counter and the wood cook stove were removed to the back porch, along with the pieces of Papa's bedstead. The back room became a library full of dark, gleaming shelves. The door to my bedroom, slated to become the upstairs parlor, now stretched into a broad archway. Near dusk, when all the workers had left, Kelda would proudly display the progress. I watched with an element of sadness as every vestige of my home—the only home I had ever known—was discarded like an unfashionable garment.

Allen asked Kelda to choose the furniture for the entire place. Everything was to look first-class. She would select the fabrics and the styles for the draperies that I was to sew. The whole family, excluding Dieter and myself, spent four days shopping in Superior.

Onkel Peter had sent Papa a telegram about the sale. During the trip, he arranged for the cash to be sent by the Wells Fargo Bank in Superior. Katrina looked for new furniture for her house in Cloquet, while Kelda and Allen—with Tante Janna as a chaperone—traipsed from one shop to another ordering fabric, wallpaper, furniture, and carpets.

While they were gone, Dieter and I moved Papa's bedstead up to my attic bedroom. I salvaged the garden tools from the cellar. They now stood in a clutter by the stairwell. The counter, the cook stove, and the ice chest from the cellar were all too bulky for me to move. I posted a notice of sale in Tucker's Dry Goods store and was able to sell the items that way. It felt so good to have money again!

The letter from Lars sat on the sideboard for two weeks before Kelda opened it. Every day I prayed for Lars. I knew by experience the disappointment he would feel.

I felt shame at Kelda's behavior. I never saw her show regret, nor did I see the courtesy of reply. I hoped that she had privately mailed a brief explanation of her sudden change of mind. The day that I found all of Lars' letters in the trash, I wrote a long letter to Papa detailing the family's activities. I figured that Lars would find out indirectly, in a gentler manner, if he hadn't already found his answer through Kelda's silence.

I salvaged those letters from the trash, but I dared not read them. I fingered the script on the envelopes, treasuring the memory of its source, but I feared to know the contents. After two days of agony and temptation, I burned them in the pot-bellied stove. They were all I had of Lars, but they weren't mine. I didn't want the burden of their secrets.

15: The Wrong Choice

The summer months passed quickly. Between sewing drapes for a dozen windows and planting Tante Janna's garden, I hardly found time to clean the attic. The Nelson house buzzed with activity. The trip to Superior proved a clandestine mission for Allen Hollings. He had purchased a sapphire engagement ring, which he presented to Kelda a week later, after a long consultation with Onkel Peter.

What a couple they made! His dark, striking features blazed beside her fair, captivating beauty. Everyone commented on how good Kelda and Allen looked together, on how perfect they were for each other. Allen dressed expensively; his wardrobe easily matched Kelda's in quantity and quality. His social graces blended well with hers. His wealth and education befitted her standing. She was, after all, the doctor's daughter. He treated her like a queen, almost bragging about how he'd fallen in love with his "goddess" the moment he saw her.

Kelda's face glowed with happiness. She was settling in her new furniture, ordering her trousseau, and planning her wedding all at once. She and Tante Janna traveled to Superior a second time and returned with a load of expensive fabrics. After all my other work, I sat up late sewing for her, missing the pleasant chats we used to have when I had first sewn for her in my attic room. Now Allen filled her days. She had no use for my company.

I had plenty of time to think as I worked. I wanted to be happy for Kelda, but I felt uneasy. Was I merely envious of her success? Was I jealous of Allen's affection, having met him first? Or had the anger over how she must surely have hurt Lars seeped into my soul and poisoned it? Something about their whirlwind romance bothered me, but I couldn't pinpoint the source. Was it the whirlwind itself? Or was it my meanness?

The garden behind the shop had been trampled by workmen. I rose at four one morning to transplant the remains of Mamma's perennials to the back of Tante Janna's garden, afraid that they would be ruined beyond recovery. Among the plants were Adelle's strawberries. They bore two gallons of berries that summer. I dug out the recipe Adelle had copied for me, quivering with memories. I thought of Lars and his joke about that jar of jam that I owed him. He had never collected it. I wondered if he even remembered.

Slowly, a plan formulated in my mind. Now that I had a little money, life was filled with possibilities. I bought two dozen pint jars, packed in a crate with a wooden grid. As summer progressed, I dragged Dieter and Kirsten on one fruit-hunt after another. We picked blueberries, blackberries, raspberries, wild grapes, crab apples, and dark red cherries. I made jams and jellies. I filled every one of those jars and sealed them with wax.

By the middle of August, all but two jars were stashed in a crate addressed to Papa, the empty slots filled with waxed-paper packages of chocolate fudge. As caution against breakage, I wrapped the crate in the wool quilt I had finished, the one made up of puffy dark squares. I bought a thick navy cotton flannel that had just arrived at Tucker Dry Goods and made sheets and pillowcases for Papa's bed. I shipped everything in a crate to Papa.

I kept back one jar of blackberry jam and one of strawberry jam. I buried those at the bottom of Mamma's trunk, in case Lars ever tried to collect.

I made a point of writing to Papa every week, but I hadn't let slip a word about this surprise. Oh, it felt good to have money to spend! Papa had been writing once a month with an update of the progress. With the money from the sale of the shop in Ashland, he had been able to hire a crew to dig a cellar and frame up both the shop and the church, and that's where the work had stopped.

He was living in the cellar of the shop structure now, for it offered more work area than the room at Mrs. Higdon's, and of course it didn't cost extra money every week. But he said it wasn't fit for me. He disliked his own cooking.

There were no windows or doors hung yet. Lars was supposed to build those when he was done with Katrina's house. I wondered when that would be.

In September, after I had finished sewing clothes for Kelda and the rest of the family, I removed the bolt of cream-colored silk from inside my mattress and made myself three shirtwaists, each of a different pattern.

One had a simple, rounded neckline and a lovely v-shaped inset of sheer embroidered fabric left over from Kelda's wedding dress. Another had a high collar and rows upon rows of vertical pleats. The last had a pointed collar with a wide plum ribbon.

With the remaining silk, I made myself luxurious undergarments—a chemise, three camisoles trimmed with lavender flowerets and satin ribbon, and bloomers to match.

Of all Mamma's fabrics, only two bolts were left—a soft brown worsted wool and a burgundy corduroy. From those I cut two more suits for myself. I planned to wear the burgundy corduroy at Kelda's fall wedding. There were enough scraps of pastel cottons to form two more shirtwaists—one pale pink, one blue. I finished my clothes in secret, working at night, and stored them in Mamma's chest, satisfied that I now possessed three complete new outfits for Cloquet.

I had not heard from Papa lately, but the day before Katrina's child was born, a telegram arrived, sending for me. My heart leaped with gratitude, though I dared not show it. I felt guilty about wanting to leave so badly. Though I could justify my reasons to myself, I feared Tante Janna might accuse me of ingratitude for so readily wishing to depart her company.

Nils had wired a message to Katrina as well. He wanted her to return with me as soon as she could manage the trip, for I could help her with the children. Eager to see her husband and her new home, she made plans to travel a few days after Kelda's October wedding. Tante Janna thoroughly disapproved of traveling with a newborn infant, but Katrina had made up her mind.

The night of Elmer's birth I will never forget. Despite the crisp air, I had left the attic window open six inches. At Katrina's first cry, I woke up, curled in a ball, shivering under the quilts. I shut the window and lay there listening.

I was used to the whip of the wind around the roof, to the creaks and groans of the house. I was not used to Katrina's groans.

Mamma had never told me what childbirth was like. I didn't have the slightest clue of the pain it entailed. I lay awake and prayed, remembering the stillborn birth of Katrina's second child.

Then Tante Janna called for me. I boiled hot water for her. I emptied and scrubbed the chamber pot. I carried the sleeping Dieter from his cot up to my bed. I boiled more water. I emptied the washbasin and two buckets and refilled them with hot water. Tante Janna moved back and forth between the screens that Onkel Peter had set up, giving me instructions.

In between errands, I stood in the doorway, marveling at this miracle of womanhood. *Will I ever experience its agonies and joys? Will I have all this wonderful help? How would I handle the pain?*

I heard Tante Janna's and Onkel Peter's voices soothing and encouraging; Katrina's screams; Elmer's squall. When Tante Janna brought him bundled up, red and wrinkled and bloody, I thought something was wrong with him.

Onkel Peter laughed. "You have never seen a newly born baby, have you?"

"But his head is squeezed out of shape, Onkel Peter!" I protested, my brows knit with worry. I was glad Tante Janna was holding him. He looked so fragile.

"He'll mend," Onkel Peter said with a smile.

*   *   *

Kelda's wedding was set for ten days later, on Saturday, October 12, 1889. Tante Janna became crazed with the idea of having the house perfect for the wedding. She handled the decorations, but cleaning became my task. As I scrubbed everything ceiling to floor, I mentally planned for the trip.

How would I move all my treasures stored in the attic? I had saved the exquisite scraps from Kelda's trousseau and earlier orders to make a lovely crazy quilt. I hadn't had time to make one, but it pained me to leave those lovely pieces behind.

Mamma's trunk could not contain everything. I'd have to find crates to pack the bedding, dishes, and goods in the cupboard. We would need those things in Cloquet. I couldn't imagine how Papa managed without them. I made a mental note to beg a crate from Mrs. Tucker on every trip to the general store.

When the house sparkled with cleanliness, Kelda drafted me to put Allen Hollings' office and their new apartment in polished order before the big event. Allen had been living there for nearly two months, having moved out of his expensive suite at the Chequamegon Hotel as soon as the workers finished.

Cleaning up after him ought to be Kelda's work, I groused. *She's the one marrying him.* Her imposition took true gall, I told myself. Kelda never seemed to consider my feelings when making her plans.

I consented nonetheless. I didn't want to make trouble. I mopped the layer of dust off the newly varnished floors and washed and ironed and folded Allen's clothes. I washed a pile of cups and plates and changed the sheets on the unmade bed.

Then trouble came to me anyway. There, amidst the covers, I found something that evoked in me a pity for Kelda that I never thought possible—a pair of bloomers. They weren't Kelda's. I would have recognized those since I had been doing all the laundry for the Nelson family for months.

I recognized the bloomers. I had made them: silk bloomers edged with pink embroidered rosebuds. They belonged to the wife of the man who managed the Chequamegon Hotel. Allen Hollings was apparently not the gentleman he appeared to be.

Restlessness and worry vexed me. *What should I do? Kelda must be told, but if I tell her, would she believe me?* There were only a few days before the wedding. I knew my cousin. Even if she weren't head-over-heels in love, she would not want to face the shame of calling off the wedding. She wouldn't want to admit she didn't really know the man to whom she was committing her future.

For months now I had managed to interact with her amiably, but there was still that edge of criticism beyond her words, the air of disdain. In my wildest imaginations, I could picture her accusing me of jealousy, of wanting to destroy her marriage to a wealthy and handsome man, or worse yet—of planting the bloomers there myself. She would rub in the fact that I would never rate his attention, much less that of others.

I agonized over what to do. I could bring the evidence to Onkel Peter or Tante Janna. Surely they would be objective enough to understand—or better yet, Katrina.

I felt responsible for saving Kelda from sorrow, but would knowledge of my findings do that? People often saw only what they wanted to see, hence the old sayings "Love is blind" and "Hope springs eternal in the human heart."

Don't we always hope for the best despite negative signs? Hadn't I myself done so with Lars? I had thought he liked me.

I understood then what had bothered me about Kelda's relationship. She had rushed into this arrangement without careful observation and analysis.

She couldn't have known how Allen had looked at me before he saw her, and how quickly he had changed the object of his charm. He was a ladies' man. While Kelda was with him, she commanded his attention, but out of her presence, he apparently worked his charm on more convenient women. And Kelda was clueless.

Would she see now? I doubted she would, but certainly *I* could learn from her mistakes. I would observe in silence long before I accepted any offer of marriage. I would garner the perspectives of others. Oh, if only I in my self-righteous reasoning had turned to God in prayer! But seeking God's leading about this matter never occurred to me for some reason.

In the end, to my own discredit, I decided to do nothing. I was afraid that the whole affair would be thrown back in my face, that Kelda would accuse me of doing the unthinkable.

Yet the unthinkable was exactly what I ended up doing, in a twisted sort of way. I washed and pressed the fine silk bloomers I'd found and made a matching camisole, replete with pink embroidered rosebuds. I wrapped them as a wedding present.

The gift I had planned for Kelda—a sleeveless silk nightgown, edged with expensive French lace and fastened with three pearl buttons—I stashed in Mamma's trunk. I had made it with the last of Mamma's cream-colored silk and the leftover trim from Kelda's wedding dress. In my opinion, it was too good to be enjoyed by the likes of Allen Hollings.

I never witnessed the ceremony. We had spent the week before baking enough to feed an army, but I still barely escaped from the kitchen in time to change. I had hurriedly donned the burgundy suit, but when I arrived at the base of the stairs, Katrina thrust Elmer into my arms with a plea to keep him quiet.

The parlor was already crowded with guests. I took him upstairs to the attic and changed back into a work dress. I can't say that I regretted missing the vows, knowing what I did.

I had left my gift on the table with those of others. Allen swept Kelda away before she could open gifts. Onkel Peter, Dieter, and I carried them to the apartment above the shop. Tante Janna promptly went to bed while I stayed up to finish the dishes and straighten the house.

On Sunday I took extra pains to look nice. This would be my last service in our Norwegian Lutheran church.

I wore the plum-colored suit and hat, along with the plain-collared shirtwaist and a plum-colored ribbon. I fixed my hair in a French braid with the end tucked up and under, making the braid fuller. I surveyed the results in the mirror. In the morning sunlight, the plum-colored suit looked more the color of blackberry syrup.

When he saw me, Onkel Peter swept his hat off his silver curls and bowed. "Annetti, you've grown into a young woman right before our eyes."

"*Ja*, I was wondering when you would finally wear that hat," Tante Janna added, adjusting the brim of hers as she stared into the hall mirror. She smiled at Onkel Peter's reflection in the mirror. She may have looked pale and tired, but her beauty still held his eye.

I smiled, not knowing what to think. I'd been a young woman for quite some time now, and nobody had noticed in the least. My seventeenth birthday had slipped by, unnoticed during the whirlwind preparations for Kelda's wedding. Two unnoticed birthdays! Then worse thoughts filled my mind:

Not another word from Tante Janna. Couldn't she have been gracious enough to admit that with a bit of attention, I could look something close to beautiful? Or at least fair? Ah! But Onkel Peter never suggested I was beautiful. Wise man that he was, he only remarked on my growing up.

Oh, why do I have to notice such details and torture myself with them? Why am I so cynical? Just admit it, Annetti! You don't rate in a household full of gorgeous women.

Still, I thought, Papa would have teased me about how good I looked. Oh, how I missed his cheerful banter!

Adelle stopped me after church, an act that startled me. During Kelda's correspondence with Lars, Kelda had often managed to catch Lars' family after church and spend some time visiting with Adelle. I had made a point of keeping my distance, not wishing fresh pain, usually excusing myself immediately after the service to rush back to Tante Janna's to start dinner.

My absence had not kept me from glancing discreetly at Lars' family during the service, however. Since my visit to the farm and Kelda's fateful introduction to Mr. Hollings, I'd seen Inga's friendly glances toward Kelda turn to yearning, disappointment, disdain, and an expression close to spite.

Kelda had never returned to the farm after that day of our visit. Mr. Hollings consumed her attention, and everyone else dropped into obscurity.

Adelle and I had not spoken in months. "You look lovely, Annetti," she began. "You always look neat and clean, but today you look especially beautiful: Your true self shines through."

I blushed under her smile, relishing the rare compliment, especially when spoken by this woman whom I had admired since that first day on the farm.

"You go to your Papa this week, *ja*? Wednesday?"

I nodded, surprised that she knew.

"I have a present to send to Lars. Can you see that it is delivered to him?"

"Yes, certainly," I replied.

"I will see that it is delivered to the train station. I am so glad that you will be there to take care of him. You know, he loved that jam." Her eyes twinkled, but she stopped abruptly when I stiffened at her words.

He loved the jam I sent to Papa? Why hadn't I heard from him then? Or from Papa?

Her blue eyes pierced through me, and she spoke with an odd mixture of both sternness and compassion: "Forgive him, Annetti. He is a good man at heart."

"What do you mean, 'Take care of him'?" I stammered, still mentally stuck on her first lines. "Will Lars be boarding with us again?" I bristled with annoyance that I seemed to be the last one to be informed of decisions.

My face must have registered my thoughts as her other words sank in. "And for what must I forgive him?" My tone was cold.

Adelle looked at me strangely, a faraway look in her azure eyes. "It is not for me to say, Annetti. But I tell you something you must remember. God knows our frame. He made us. He understands that we are only dust, full of weaknesses and sin. And when we do wrong, God forgives our sin when we ask. He puts our sin as far away as the east is from the west."

I stood astonished and perplexed. A sick feeling sank into my gut at the mention of weaknesses and wrongdoing and sin. I thought of the bloomers in Allen's bed and of my fear of confronting that issue with Kelda and her family.

Adelle spoke again, looking deep into my eyes. "Annetti, you must forgive as God forgives. Do not judge others, for that is God's job. So is revenge. God knows everything, and He will repay accordingly."

My whole body drooped then. I realized I'd sat in judgment on Kelda and Tante Janna and Onkel Peter. Papa and Lars too. *Who was I to usurp God's job?*

She smiled gently now and patted my hand. "*Ja*, forgive him, Annetti, and anyone else who does not deserve your kindness. Do it for your own soul." With that, she disappeared.

Questions raced through my mind. *Had she read my thoughts? What had Lars done that warranted my forgiveness? Had she finally realized that I had read the personal postscript in Lars' letter? But that was months ago! Why would it matter now?*

I stood frozen in thought. Onkel Peter had to call me twice before I heard him.

Sunday afternoon was quiet. At Tante Janna's insistence, Onkel Peter took the family out to eat at the Chequamegon Hotel. I begged off, not wanting him to spend unnecessary money on my account and not wishing to chance accosting the manager's wife and making the mistake of judging her. I walked home alone and packed myself a picnic lunch.

I spent a long while at Mamma's grave. I'd seen so many changes since her death a year and a half ago! I thought about Adelle's advice and the cryptic plea for forgiveness.

Lord, someday let me know what to say and speak with confidence as she does, I prayed. Tante Janna was a lady, but she could not compare with Adelle's wise, indomitable spirit.

Life at Tante Janna's house now seemed dull, even with Dieter around. We had enough food left over from the wedding that no one needed to cook.

Tante Janna spent most of her time in bed, pensive and depressed. I waited on her, bringing tea and buttered toast, worried about her. Had she somehow found out about Allen Hollings when they had dinner at the hotel? Is that what consumed her thoughts?

Onkel Peter assured me that Tante Janna would be fine. Physical exhaustion could be cured with plenty of rest. She simply needed time to recuperate from the months of excitement over Elmer's birth and Kelda's wedding. He promised her spirits would rise as she gained strength. I clung to his optimism.

I felt the pangs of guilt again. I would be leaving Tante Janna soon, and the horror of a marriage broken before it was bound would surface eventually, making Tante Janna's depression worse. I grieved when Tante Janna and Katrina exchanged harsh words over the date set for traveling—Wednesday. But I was glad that I would accompany Katrina. I longed to see Papa. Weeks had flown by without as much as a postcard from him.

Cleaning and packing consumed my time during the next few days. I had hung up bunches of herbs and flower blossoms to dry among the rafters. Savoring the fragrant mint, I now bundled it in brown paper. I wrapped the other herbs and the flower seeds in turn, marking each packet carefully, imagining the fine garden I would plant behind Papa's shop.

After rearranging the contents of Mamma's trunk, I decided to use a crate to ship the fabric scraps that filled it. I would pack Mamma's dishes in the trunk, among my clothes, providing a cushion. The two jars of jam were still stashed at the bottom.

I walked to the train station and arranged for my passage and the shipping of our household goods. I hired a wagon and two men to move the furniture and the pot-bellied stove. The cost ate up every cent I had left.

Tante Janna nearly sent the movers away. "We do not have that much luggage that we need a wagon. There must be some mistake! We are not paying for a wagon."

"I am, Tante Janna," I intervened. Turning to the men, I told them, "You'll find the trunks and furniture on the third floor. You can't miss them. They're stacked in the empty attic."

Tante Janna fell back into the overstuffed chair in the parlor, stunned. "And how do you pay them? Honestly, Annetti—I thought that you would stay. What is there in Cloquet?! Nothing! Katrina would not go if Nils had not insisted. I never thought she would go through with the trip, not so soon after Elmer's birth."

"There is my Papa, Tante Janna. I want to be with Papa in Cloquet. He sent for me. The money for the shipping came from the sale of the store counter and Mamma's kitchen stove and ice chest." I held my breath, hoping she wouldn't accuse me of stealing.

Tante Janna just stared at me. "But I am used to all of your help! How will I ever do without you? I would have to hire two maids. That we cannot afford!"

I cringed inside. Had I meant only that much to Tante Janna during the last ten months?

She'd miss my work, but not me—not her niece? An edge of fury crept inside me. *Did she think she owned me? And who was she to counter the authority of Papa's telegram?*

"Judge not, that you be not judged," a voice repeated in my mind. "Vengeance belongs to God, who knows all things." The memory of Adelle's voice calmed my soul. "The Lord knows that we are all made of dust, and yet he forgives us of all our sins."

I bit my tongue and stood silent, fighting to paste a genuinely kind smile on my face. "Forgive all the people who do not deserve your kindness," Adelle had said. *Had she known?*

Compassion for Tante Janna crept slowly into my heart. She had always carried herself with poise. Countless times over, she'd proven herself a congenial and gracious mother and hostess. But now she was crumbling like a clod of dirt squeezed in someone's fist. *The Lord knows our frame, and He loves us anyway,* I thought. *Let me understand and love too.*

"Of course she must go, Janna." Onkel Peter slipped his arm around my shoulders and looked down at me. "Annetti has been a double blessing to our family, but she deserves a life of her own. She deserves to see her father. Her mother would want her to go."

Tante Janna's plump figure sprawled across the parlor chair, frozen stiff. She stared at Onkel Peter and then at me.

"You look like your mother once did, before she married your Papa. I could not stop her then either, though I tried to make her see that she should marry a man who can make a decent living." An edge of disdain accompanied her voice.

My mother! Here was a story that I had not heard! *Tante Janna hadn't wanted Mamma to marry my father?* But I dared not ask more.

"Thank you, Onkel Peter." I gave him a quick hug. Then I crossed the room and knelt before her. "Dear Tante Janna, I love my Papa. Though he may not be worthy in your eyes, I think… I think there are perhaps far more important things in life than making a decent living."

"You are your mother all over again," she said evenly, pulling a folded bill from her coin purse. "Here. You will need this."

I stared, unmoving. A crisp five-dollar bill lay creased in her outreached hand. *Was this a test, a test of the values I had just stated?* I hesitated to take it.

"Here," she said, shoving the bill into my hand. "It is yours. Your Papa sent it for you."

Numbly, I took the bill, wondering what she would have done with it if I had consented to stay.

I wanted to shudder, but instead I embraced her. Though reluctant and disapproving, she was releasing me to a life of joy with Papa. She had given up the money so important to her. I thought of Adelle's words: "Forgive. Forgive for the sake of your own soul."

Oh, God, let my life be full of forgiveness like Yours!

"Thank you, Tante Janna! Oh, thank you so much!" I hugged her tight, but she didn't respond in kind. Her body was stiff. I dropped my arms and backed off. "Excuse me. I forget myself." I turned and headed up the stairs.

"I would be wrong not to thank *you*, Annetti," she called after me, a bit harshly but without contempt. "We have appreciated all your hard vurk."

I wore Mamma's old black muslin dress and the old brown coat for traveling, as Katrina had told me that our clothes would likely be covered with soot from the engine. The dress smelled faintly of pine cleaner, as I had worn it the previous day, when I had scrubbed every inch of the attic one last time and stacked my belongings at the top of the stairs.

Dieter, clad in his every-day play clothes and a canvas jacket lined with flannel, was put in my charge, along with the basket of lunch. Katrina carried Elmer and a large bag full of his things. She wore a faded blue gown beneath her old blue wool cape. Though plump, she still looked stunning—both lovely and vivacious.

Except for the cool breeze, we couldn't have asked for a more pleasant day for traveling.

Tante Janna still fretted over Katrina: "So soon after the delivery? She is barely recovered! Little Elmer is two weeks old!"

Onkel Peter shook his silver curls and sighed. "She can't stay away from her husband forever, can she, Janna? Nils has been patient enough already. The house is finished. They're snug for winter. It's better for her to travel now, before winter sets in. She is young and strong. She has Annetti there to help her. What more can we ask?"

Katrina chimed in. "I'll be just fine, Mamma. You still have Kirsten to look after, and it's time for her to begin helping you with more of the work. She'll be a young lady soon. She needs to learn as I did. Why, you had me scrubbing floors when I was barely six!"

I followed the movers to the train station to make sure everything was in order. The crates for Lars had arrived. So many! I wondered what was in them. Fortunately, Adelle had paid the shipping charges.

At the station, Tante Janna was full of tearful goodbyes. She hovered about Dieter and Katrina, hugging them countless times. Every other word was a piece of advice about what to do or not do on the train. To her credit, Katrina bore the ordeal patiently.

Tante Janna hugged me last. "Thank God, you are strong, Annetti! Take good care of Katrina and Dieter—little Elmer too."

"I will, Tante Janna. I won't let them out of my sight. Goodbye, Onkel Peter! Thank you for letting me stay in your home for so long after Papa left." He shook my hand and nodded.

We boarded the train and took our seats. I sat amid the crowd, among my relatives, feeling alone. I had not been truly ignored, but no one had fussed or worried over me at this final goodbye. Perhaps they didn't worry because I was strong. Or because they knew Papa would be there waiting for me.

There was a time after Mamma's death when I hadn't considered myself strong at all. Was being strong a blessing? It didn't seem so in ways. It meant bearing more work.

Tante Janna expected me to take care of Katrina and Dieter. Adelle seemed to think I should take care of Lars. Papa wanted me to take care of him. He hated cooking and the endless housework that kept him from stitching up orders.

Who will take care of me? I wondered. The thought made me ache inside.

16: Anna Skagerberg

It was raining when we arrived—a cold rain that pounded the station awning stretched across the tracks. Dieter sat with his nose pasted to the steamy window as we waited to disembark. All the way from Duluth he had quizzed me about our arrival.

I had patiently explained that his Papa as well as mine would be there when we arrived. We had sent Nils a telegram from the depot in Duluth. His Papa would come with a big wagon to haul our luggage. He would cover it with an oiled canvas tarp to protect it from the rain. By late tonight, Dieter would be sleeping in his own bed, in his very own room inside his new house.

Dieter still worried. "It's too dark. I can't see them!" he protested. Then in nearly the same breath, he let out a screech and yelled, "Papa!"

Katrina caught my eye and laughed. She was in a good mood since Elmer had slept most of the day. She had even been able to doze off herself, for after lunch she had tucked Elmer into the open half of the picnic basket on the empty seat beside her. Dieter had drifted off too, his head in my lap. Only I had remained awake. I stifled a yawn and stood to stretch. We were all tired of sitting.

I carried the empty picnic basket and the bag of Elmer's things, along with a satchel of my own. As Nils marvelled over his new son and hugged Dieter and Katrina, I searched for a familiar face in the yellow lights.

Where is Papa?

I glanced back at Nils and Katrina. His curly head bent down toward her upturned face. Their conversation appeared intimate but serious. Katrina looked grave but nodded at me when I caught her eye. She gave me a look of pity.

I felt a sick, gnawing feeling in my stomach. *What was it Adelle couldn't tell me? Was it something Nils was telling Katrina now? Lars must have written to Adelle about something that warranted my forgiveness.* I pushed away the panic that threatened to overwhelm me.

"Is there something wrong?" I asked loudly. Papa should be here. Do you know where he is, Nils?" My voice wavered.

"He was not feeling well, Annetti. He needs to stay out of the rain and the cold. I will see that your baggage is delivered." He left before I could ask anything more of him.

We headed inside the depot to wait. Katrina avoided my questioning eyes. By the time Nils returned, the rain had slowed to a drizzle.

"We will ride in the wagon with the baggage," Nils told us. With a grin, he produced an umbrella. "But I have this—a loan from the station master."

Katrina slipped one hand through the crook of his elbow, cradling Elmer in her other arm. Dieter clung to Nils' umbrella arm. I trailed behind in the drizzle, carrying the bags. Nils helped Katrina up to the driver's bench and deposited Dieter in back of the wagon. Without a word, I deposited the bags and climbed in with Dieter. We sat among the crates and the furniture. Two deliverymen with lanterns sat at the rear. We slipped under the tarp to avoid the drizzle. It smelled of oil and sweat.

"Isn't this fun, Annetti?" Dieter asked, grinning. "Mamma told me this is Indian country." He peeked from beneath the tarp. "But I don't see any Indians yet."

"You're on watch, Dieter. Let me know when you see one."

We passed warehouses and factories along the river. Then the wagon swung left and rumbled up a hill. The Clydesdales snorted and strained at the weight. The furniture shifted, and the men scrambled to steady the load.

Up, up, up we went, until we levelled off and swung left. Then we turned right into a circular driveway. Dieter threw back his corner of the tarp.

"Are we home?" he asked eagerly.

"*Ja*," Nils answered. "Home."

I clambered out of the wagon and stood in the drizzle. The soft lights from the house streamed across a flat, open yard. The house looked familiar, built in the same style as the home of Tante Janna and Onkel Peter but without the attached clinic. Nils hurried us inside while the men followed with Katrina's trunk and valise.

"Where do you want the rest of the load?" one of the men asked.

"At the shop across from the church," Nils replied. "Lars will be there to help unload."

"Is that where Papa is?" I asked. I hadn't wanted to face Lars, at least not so soon—not like this, in Mamma's old black muslin dress and my old winter coat.

"*Ja*, but wait until morning. Katrina is tired. You must be too. Sleep here tonight."

I was indeed tired—too exhausted to argue. As I took off my wraps, I heard Katrina's exclamations of delight from the parlor. I followed Nils there.

"It is a dream, Nils," she gushed happily. "It's just like my parents' home. It even has the furniture I admired in Superior. How did you know?"

"Compliments of your parents," Nils explained. "They had it shipped from Superior after the house was finished." He took us on a tour. Pillars, porch, Palladian windows, even the oval glass in the front door looked the same.

In the kitchen, a freshly built fire roared in the wood stove, and tea simmered on the back burner. We sat to enjoy a cup before exploring the upstairs. Katrina sat in the kitchen rocker, nursing Elmer, with an extra blanket cozily draped over both of them.

"What a treat! Someone has been expecting us," I remarked aloud, lifting the cover of the teapot and sniffing the fragrant brew. "A cozy fire and fresh tea—you must have a good friend."

"Anna Skagerberg," Nils and Katrina repeated together at once, laughing at their simultaneous response.

"Well, she must be a dear to think of such comforts."

Katrina positioned Elmer across her shoulder. "Poor fellow. He's fallen asleep again." She patted his back until he burped. "I think you'll find there is no one quite like Anna Skagerberg," she told me with a smile of intrigue. "I imagine you'll meet her soon enough."

Dieter had fallen asleep over his tea. Nils carried him upstairs. Katrina and I followed.

Two of the four bedrooms were furnished with big four-poster beds, dressers, washstands, lamps, and chamber pots. Katrina and Nils' room also boasted a large wool carpet and a polished rocking chair and curtains and a crib for Elmer too. Warmth emanated from the kitchen below.

I wondered where I would sleep tonight. I leaned against the doorway, watching.

Nils sat on the big bed with Dieter against his shoulder, talking with Katrina while she sat in the rocker. He beamed at her beautiful face, clearly glowing with joy over their new home and reunited family. They looked so happy.

A knock sounded below. Both Katrina and Nils laughed.

"That would be Anna, my guess," Katrina said with a grin. "Would you mind?"

"Of course not," I answered, descending the darkened stairs with a cautious step. I found Anna framed by the oval glass of the front door, a dark shadow so short that it could have been made by a child. I rushed to let her in.

"Katri—" she began as I held open the storm door for her, but she stopped short when her glance met mine. "You must be Annetti."

My eyes widened in surprise. "Yes. Katrina predicted you would be Anna Skagerberg. I'm glad to meet you!" I followed her to the kitchen. She seemed to know exactly where to go with the large pot she carried. Wisps of steam slipped from the edges of its cover. I smelled its heady fragrance, now more overcome with hunger than with exhaustion.

She set the pot on the stove and pulled two loaves of fresh bread from the canvas bag slung over her shoulder. "There!" she stated in Norwegian. "Glad to meet you too. My husband Elon and I run a boarding house not far from your Papa's shop. Nils and Katrina used to board with us before they built their house. Your father used to eat with us, though he lodged in that cheap pigsty run by Mrs. Higdon."

I looked at her, alarmed. "Used to? Surely he still eats!"

She peered at me, her wrinkled face registering vexation. "I assume he eats," she snapped. "But he's been ill. Lars brings him food now."

"Ill? I've heard nothing of that. Ill with what?"

"Ill in the head, if you ask me. I've never met a man more stubborn than Andrew Sorenson. Gives half his fortune to build a church but refuses the kindness of his neighbors, of everyone except Lars and once in a while Nils. You do know Lars, don't you?"

I nodded uncertainly.

Her gray eyes twinkled. "That is good news, indeed! That poor boy needs a good wife."

I blushed. "You were telling me about Papa."

"Your Papa can do his own telling," she declared firmly. "I want to hear about Lars. How well do you know him?"

I had found a knife to slice the bread, but now I froze. *Her question could be taken two ways: How trustworthy is Lars, or how close a friend is he?* Both questions made me blush.

"Aha! I knew it! You are the beauty who broke his heart, aren't you? And now you've come because you're sorry?"

Her accusation roused me. *What a gossip! I'll have to set her straight.* I took a deep breath and faced her. "Mrs. Skagerberg, I'm rather plain, don't you think? Not a beauty at all. And as for breaking Lars' heart, I would have had to win his heart first. My cousin Kelda did that. Kelda is Katrina's younger sister."

I finished my speech and sliced the bread, but her eyes bore a hole into me. Her silence seemed to demand more explanation.

"I had a telegram from Papa about two weeks ago," I offered. "It said that I should join him. Finally! He had written to me every few weeks at first, but as the summer wore on, he wrote less and less. He didn't mention your name, but I knew that Lars was working on this house as well as the shop. Apparently—"

I paused to consider my wording and check my tone; I did not wish to sound disrespectful—especially not to someone kind enough to feed us. "Apparently, there is a great deal that my father never told me. You seem to know things that I haven't learned yet."

Mrs. Skagerberg studied me closely as I rummaged through the sideboard to find flatware and napkins. The lively expressions on her wrinkled face amused me: her eyebrows twitched with understanding, her head tilted to one side. She held her mouth in a thoughtful pucker.

"So how well do you know Lars?" she persisted.

There was that question again. I tried to skirt it by changing the subject: "You don't know how much all of us appreciate your kindness in bringing over a meal, Mrs. Skagerberg. I'm sure Katrina would love to have you eat with us. Shall I set a place for you?"

She appeared surprised. She shook her head and spoke only one word: "Lars."

I sighed and shrugged. "There's not much to say. He ate his meals with us for a few months, and Papa rented the back room to him for his carpentry work."

I paused. "He travelled to Cloquet with Papa, and they both rented the room from Mrs. Higdon."

"Lena Higdon," she spit out scornfully. "That woman—"

I cut her off before she could continue. "Papa mentioned Lars in his letters occasionally, mostly in conjunction with the shop or the church."

"Ah! Well! So you're not the fair-haired young lady he's been pining for, but you might do anyway," Anna insisted.

I looked up, startled. *Was she trying to set me up? Was Lars still pining for Kelda after all these months? He must have truly loved her if he still pined for her so!*

I swallowed with difficulty. "*Ja*, well then, I am obviously not fair-haired. My hair is brown. As I said, Lars was fond of my cousin Kelda, who does indeed have blond hair. Curly blond hair. She's beautiful, like Katrina. They wrote to each other for several months."

In my mind's eye, I could envision that last letter sitting on the kitchen shelf for two weeks before Kelda opened it. The hurt inside me stung like a scab pried off before it's loose.

"And what happened?" She was eyeing me closely, studying my every reaction.

I walked around her and began setting the table, willing myself to speak in a disinterested, objective tone. "Allen Hollings happened. He moved to Ashland to set up an office as an attorney. He bought Papa's shop, with the living quarters above, and asked Kelda to decorate them."

"I think it may have been love at first sight. For Kelda, nothing else seemed to matter. It was like she forgot about Lars. Allen and Kelda were married recently. I suspect that Kelda never wrote Lars about any of that."

Anna frowned. "That boy needs a good wife to take care of him. Pound some sense in him too. Tch! I wouldn't have to scold him so much if he had a wife."

I raised my eyebrows at the term "boy," wondering what Lars would have thought of her choice of words. *Boy? He was twenty-seven, ten years older than I.*

A smile twitched at my lips. "Come, now, Mrs. Skagerberg," I said with a chuckle. "I suspect you rather enjoy a good scolding. Though how you can scold and yet be such a good-hearted dear as to look after our supper—well, you amaze me."

Fortunately, Katrina appeared in the doorway then carrying Elmer. Of course, the sleeping babe had to be admired and adored and Katrina's health discussed. Nils appeared and explained that Mrs. Skagerberg's cooking had kept him in good health. I learned that she and her husband Elon lived partway down the hill on Avenue G, not far from the back side of the church.

We enjoyed Anna's vegetable soup and fresh bread. When I found my eyes drooping, I excused myself and offered to tuck Elmer into the crib in the big bedroom. After getting him settled, I peeked into Dieter's room. He lay curled in a ball, a small lump under the quilts of the big bed.

Bone-tired, I clumsily shed the black muslin, loosened the covers from the foot of the bed and crawled in opposite Dieter, clad in my petticoats. I fell asleep praying for Papa—Papa who was ill, too ill to walk to a boarding house to eat a meal.

17: Papa

The dream seemed so real. Mamma stood on the steps of the little white church in Ashland, waving at Papa, beckoning him to join her. She held the door ajar with one hand while Papa climbed the stairs. I heard his footsteps and watched as he passed through.

"No!" I screamed. "Don't leave me!"

But Papa never looked back. Mamma didn't seem to hear either. I tried to run after them, but someone held me back, grasping my arm so hard that it hurt.

My terror jerked me awake, and I struggled to remember where I was. My arm felt numb. I'd slept on my side so hard I'd barely moved. I felt stiff. I pushed myself up into a sitting position. *Papa,* I thought. *I must see Papa today.*

The muffled noise of someone stoking the fire in the wood stove drifted up from the kitchen. *Nils must be up,* I thought. *That's why I heard footsteps in my dream.*

I rubbed my numb arm and shook it until the feeling of pins and needles subsided. Then I pulled a clean work dress from my satchel, laced up my shoes, and trudged downstairs. I nodded to Nils as I passed through the kitchen. I took my coat off the hook and headed outside.

I followed the dirt path to the outhouse, washing my hands under the icy water of the outside pump afterward. I filled the buckets on the back porch before returning to the kitchen. I set a big pot of water to boil so that Katrina would have warm water for washing Elmer.

Nils had already started a fire in the cook stove and was stirring a pot of oatmeal.

"I thought you took your meals at Anna Skagerberg's boarding house."

"I do—and we will for a while yet, until Katrina is ready to take on the task. But I like to go in early. I don't want to wait on Anna's breakfast."

"Oh! That makes sense." I took a deep breath and tackled the fear that haunted me. "I need to know about Papa."

Nils paused a long time before answering. "He has been sick since September. Had a bad cold at first, then bronchitis. You know your Papa and his vurk. He would not stop to rest."

"And now?"

He grimaced. "Pneumonia."

I flinched. I'd heard Onkel Peter talk about patients with pneumonia. I knew it was serious, often fatal. "How come no one told me?"

"Your Papa did not want to worry you. He expected to get better, of course. Then two weeks ago, Anna Skagerberg and I decided that you should be here regardless of what he thought. We sent a telegram. The doctor—"

My eyebrows arched in surprise. "There's a doctor now?"

Nils nodded. "A French doctor. He is difficult to understand."

"And what did the doctor say?" I asked, dropping into a chair for support. My knees felt suddenly weak.

"The doctor wanted to send him to a hospital in Duluth, but he refused. Anna Skagerberg offered to attend to his needs, but he was too stubborn to accept her help. He would not leave the shop. Thank God you sent him the flannel sheets and quilt. Those at least helped."

He poured the oatmeal into a bowl and stirred in a spoonful of brown sugar. "Your father is a proud man, Annetti. He was not willing to accept help from anyone except Lars. But Lars works all day. Long days. There was only so much he could do."

"But I don't understand. Why didn't Lars contact me? If he was there and knew what was happening?"

Nils just stared at me. He never answered my question. During the awkward silence, the truth dawned on me. *That's what Adelle meant when she urged me to forgive him. But how could I ever forgive him for that? Lars should have known how serious pneumonia was. His wife had died of pneumonia!*

"Your Papa was too stubborn and proud to ask you to come, Annetti. Anna Skagerberg finally sent the telegram and told him afterward."

A stab of fear ran through me. "Will Katrina be all right without me for now?" I asked.

"She will have Anna to help her, if she needs it."

"Thank you, Nils. Thank you for your kindness and consideration—and for paying for the delivery of my things last night. How much did it cost?"

Nils shook his head. "This is not a time to be proud like your father and refuse help, especially not after all of your help on the way here. Think of it as a return favor."

"Well, I truly thank you. Thank you for everything."

After extracting directions from Nils, I slipped out and ran down the dirt road. It seemed that my whole future hung in the shadows of the gray dawn. I thought of Mamma and the dream. What would the day hold? Conscious that Lars might not expect such an early visit, I pounded the door of the shop and waited. No one answered. I tried the knob and found it unlocked.

Crates and furniture filled the front room. I picked my way through the shadowy jumble, surprised at the large array of dark fabrics sitting on long shelves. A large table divided the room in half. I spotted Papa's treadle machine and chair beneath a window. The dark bulk of his work was draped neatly over the top. *Papa! He always folded his work just so.*

I picked my way to the door near Papa's treadle machine. I found Papa lying on the floor of the kitchen, stretched on a straw-tick mattress. There was no cook stove, only a pot-bellied stove in the corner. The embers were still glowing, but the room was cold.

I knelt beside the mattress and took Papa's hand in mine. His face looked sunken. His skin looked gray, but maybe the gray light of dawn was merely casting its hue over him. "Papa, Papa!" I whispered.

He opened his eyes and blinked.

"I'm here to take care of you, Papa!"

I startled at the sound of steps outside. As I whipped around, the back door flew open, letting in a rush of cold air. Lars stood in the doorway. Neither of us said a word for a long, long moment. I couldn't see his eyes to read his reaction, for the gray light of dawn streamed in behind him and cast shadows about his face.

I glanced down at Papa. He shivered beneath the quilt.

"Shut the door!" I ordered.

Lars leaned against the door with his backside, then carried in his armload of firewood. He dumped the wood into the box beside the stove and built up the fire.

I didn't know what to say; I watched him in awkward silence, my soul begging to cry out "Why? Why didn't you tell me?" But my heart stung with too much hurt to speak.

Judge not, I heard Adelle's voice in my mind. I stared out the window in stony silence. I felt Lars' eyes on me, but I didn't turn to greet him. When he left, I crumpled by Papa's side.

He returned carrying a wash pot full of water, which he placed on the stove to heat. Then he climbed the ladder to the loft. I listened to the crackle and spit of wood burning in the stove.

Papa watched me with glazed eyes, uttering no sound but a deep cough. His limp hand lay in mine, but a half-smile twitched at the corners of his mouth. He seemed glad to see me, but his pitiful condition ripped at my heart. I couldn't hide that from him. Tears welled in my eyes. My throat ached with pain. I tried to be cheerful for his sake.

"I hear you've been more stubborn than a mule, Papa," I tried to tease, but I choked on the words and ended up begging tearfully instead: "Oh, Papa, be stubborn now and fight to live. I love you. I need you. Don't leave me alone."

Papa stirred restlessly and shivered. I pulled the covers up around his shoulders, watching with horror as a circle of dark stain grew in the middle of the quilt. A ripe odor wafted upward, making me nauseous. The sight and smell were too much for me. I grabbed my old coat and headed out the back door.

I sat on the steps of the back porch. What would I do? Papa would leave me, just as Mamma had—just as in my dream. The knot in my empty stomach grew tighter.

I stared across the grassy yard to a blue outhouse at the far corner. Blue? No one painted outhouses anything but white. I let the oddity distract me.

I followed the straw-strewn path to the water pump. Nearby was a fire pit with a grill across the top. Two large water pots sat on the grill. A laundry tub and washboard leaned against the side.

"Well," I said. "That will be handy."

I continued on toward the blue outhouse and ventured inside. A counter stretched across the wall before me. On it stood a plain white porcelain pitcher, a wash basin, and a dish of soap. A white towel and washcloth lay beside them. The floor was made of stone. Behind a wall was the toilet stall, complete with a wooden lid to keep down the stench. I had never seen an outhouse so fancy. *Whose idea it had been?*

I used the stall, washed my hands, and refilled the pitcher. Then I carried the pitcher, wash basin, soap and towel inside. It wouldn't be pleasant, but I would do what needed to be done.

Lars had descended from the loft and was testing the water temperature of the pot on the stove. The sun was beginning to rise, forcing a few weak rays through the overcast sky. Its light fell on his reddened eyes and the dull stubble on his cheeks. I halted, startled by his appearance. He looked tired and drawn, as if he had not slept for days. Despite my hurt, I pitied him.

"I need to wash your Papa now, before I leave for vurk. Is there clean bedding among your things?"

Thankful to be spared that task, I nodded and placed the wash basin on the floor near Papa's head. While Lars worked, I rummaged through the crates. I found my feather bolster and pillow, along with my sheets and blankets and quilt. I set them up next to Papa so that we could roll him onto the clean bedding.

Seeing how Papa shivered, I warmed the blankets on the stove top first. Lars had stripped the putrid union suit off Papa. I winced at Papa's nakedness and gagged at the stench, but how could I not help? He looked like a baby, an infant as helpless as Elmer. Thinking of Elmer, I tucked a warm towel between his legs and drew the blankets cozily about him.

"Thank you, Annetti," Lars said.

I turned away in silence, refusing to look him in the eye.

Lars sighed and kicked the stinking pile of bedding down a trap door. He dragged the straw mattress outside and emptied it. Then he washed his hands and disappeared.

I pulled Papa's new bed closer to the stove. The activity had worn Papa out. His breathing seemed raspy, and his lips looked parched.

"Are you thirsty, Papa?" I asked. "I'll make you some tea." I was thirsty as well. I looked through the cupboards that lined the wall below the loft. Nothing! Then I remembered Anna's boarding house. Perhaps Lars had gone there to pick up something for Papa.

Well, I can't wait!

I scrounged through the crates until I found the dried mint from Mamma's garden. I made mint tea. The kitchen had grown toasty, and I slipped off my coat.

As I waited for the tea to steep, I climbed the open staircase to the loft above the front rooms. I felt like an intruder, but wasn't this my father's house?

Another straw-tick mattress lay on the floor of the loft. A trunk stood under a dormer window, a plain trunk I had once glimpsed on a wooden handcart while berry-picking in Ashland. Atop the trunk sat a large Bible and a stack of letters tied with a thin pink ribbon. I trembled. *Surely Kelda's handwriting graced those envelopes.* Anna Skagerberg had said Lars was pining for some blond-haired beauty. My eyes squeezed shut with a sudden pain. I retraced my steps.

I propped up Papa's head and tried to spoon some warm tea into his mouth, but most of it ran down his chin. I tried sticking the spoon in farther, letting the liquid trickle down the back of his throat. He licked at the wetness but then choked. His retching cough scared me. The spoon clattered across the bare floor as I scrambled to help him sit fully upright. I held him against me, pounding his back, tears streaming down my cheeks. Finally, he must have swallowed. Both scared and thankful, I lowered him gently against the pillow.

His shallow breathing made me anxious. *Is this his end? What should I do?* I held his hand as I read aloud from Mamma's Bible and sang his favorite hymn. He relaxed and fell asleep. Cramped from sitting on the floor beside the bolster, I decided to let him rest.

"Vurk!" he had always told me. "That is what you need!" Now I aimed to take his advice. It was the least I could do to honor him. Certainly there was plenty of work. There were probably piles of laundry waiting for me in the cellar. I marched outside to find the slanted cellar doors. I found a surprisingly nice cellar with walls and floor of stone, but it stank of soiled laundry. I hauled the laundry outside and left the cellar doors open to air out the place. I started a fire below the outside grill and set the big pots of water to boil.

I rummaged through the crates looking for laundry soap until I could no longer stand the jumble. I began moving things into place. Finally—some order!

There were still several crates stacked along the shop wall. In one of them I found soap. The water pots were boiling furiously by then, both the ones outside and the one on the parlor stove inside. The kitchen windows were steamy now.

The moisture will be good for Papa's cough. Onkel Peter always prescribes that treatment for congestion.

I spent the rest of the day boiling and scrubbing soiled bedding, checking Papa off and on. His condition did not change. I filled the clotheslines outside with wet but clean bedding. I found additional lines hanging from the rafters in the cellar. Soon all the lines were full. I hadn't touched the soiled clothes. That would take another day's work.

Papa looked deplorable, but I didn't know what to do for him. I heated water for a bath, which I took in the chilly cellar, as there were no curtains on the windows upstairs. I dressed in my burgundy corduroy suit, the one I had meant to wear to Kelda's wedding, glad finally to feel presentable instead of shabby.

My stomach growled. I hadn't eaten since last night, when Anna Skagerberg had served us fresh bread and vegetable soup. *Where is the food that Lars supposedly brings Papa? No breakfast, no lunch? But then Papa could hardly swallow, much less eat. So why would Lars bring him a meal? Or maybe he expected me to do that, now that I was here.*

Papa slept with his mouth open. Despite the steamy kitchen, his lips looked cracked. I didn't dare try feeding him more tea. So I moistened a cloth with warm water, wet his lips, and swabbed his mouth. I hugged his listless form, watching the faint rising of his chest with each shallow breath. I sighed. *What should I do?*

I needed help. Help to set up the bed. Help to lift Papa away from the cold draught on the floor. Surely Nils would be home soon. Surely he would help me.

I put more wood on the fire, unpacked my hat and good winter coat, and followed Carleton Avenue back to Katrina's new house. I knocked and waited, but no one answered. The windows looked dark.

Where could they be?

18: Dream Come True

Dusk had already begun to settle across the town. Men straggled up the street toward the warmth of their homes, past windows glowing with cozy yellow lamplight. I traced my steps back to the shop, watching my breath form puffs of steamy mist. The temperature had fallen. Ahead, I noticed the little white Norwegian church off to the right.

Anna Skagerberg! She lives on Avenue G behind the church. Nils and Katrina and Dieter are probably there. Papa may have been too stubborn to accept help, but I won't make that mistake.

I followed Carleton Avenue to Fourth Street. I walked along the churchyard and stopped at the street behind it. Was this Avenue G? I looked around for a sign but saw none. *It must be, but which house is hers?*

"Do you need help, ma'am?" a slight, dark-haired man asked.

"I'm looking for Anna Skagerberg's house," I replied.

"The one in the middle, over there." He pointed to a square two-story house on the right side of the street. "See the men entering the door on the porch? That's Anna's boarding house."

"Thank you," I replied. Wondering what I was getting myself into, I climbed the steps to the Skagerberg home. While I debated whether to knock, another worker arrived.

"What have we here?" he asked in a loud, boisterous voice. He spoke with a heavy Irish accent. He held the door and motioned for me to enter. "A lovely lady in our presence tonight, men! Look sharp! Find her a chair!" Men scrambled at his words.

"I just need to speak with Mrs. Skagerberg," I said.

"In the kitchen, ma'am." He nodded toward the stairway that led up to a half-landing and back down into the kitchen. "But you'd best not bother her unless you plan to help."

He chuckled and winked. "Here, sit beside me." He patted a chair near the end of the long table that ran the length of the front room. Another table stretched through the dining room. There must have been thirty chairs. Thirty! Men were milling about, arguing and laughing and joking. I felt very much out of place.

The smell of pot roast sent waves of hunger through me. I felt tempted to sit down and enjoy a meal, but the vision of Papa lying wrapped in quilts on the floor prompted me to shake my head. I made my way back to the kitchen, where I found Katrina.

Dieter sat in a rocking chair holding Elmer, supported by pillows. I winked at him and ruffled his hair. Quickly, I hung my coat and hat on a hook in the back porch and made myself useful. At least I could work for my supper.

"How's your Papa?" Katrina asked when the men had finished eating and we could finally sit down ourselves.

Elmer had been passed off to his father, who stood showing him off to a crowd of stocky lumberjacks. I watched, amazed, as long as I dared. Elmer was awake and fully content in his father's strong arms. I caught sight of Lars among the men, laughing at the cheerful banter. I looked away before he saw me. Katrina repeated her question, and I sighed.

"Not good. He opened his eyes. I know he recognized me, but he has not spoken. I tried to feed him some warm tea, but he nearly choked on the spoonful."

Mrs. Skagerberg raised her eyebrow. I answered her barrage of questions.

"There is nothing to do but wait," she said. "If he is that bad, it won't be long now."

Her words made me want to hurry back to Papa, and I started to say so, but Anna wouldn't hear of it. She made me stay and eat. I felt guilty chowing down on her delicious fare while Papa languished all alone. It seemed disloyal, yet I needed nourishment.

When I disclosed the true purpose of my visit, both Mrs. Skagerberg and Katrina insisted that I would not help with the dishes. Katrina rescued Elmer from the clamorous crowd and sent me off with Nils. Lars tagged along without asking.

Together they assembled the big bed in the front room and waited while I smoothed on sheets and quilts. Then they lifted Papa from my feather bolster onto the mattress. Fortunately, the feather bolster was still clean, though the towel between his legs needed changing. I slid the feather bolster beneath Papa's bed thinking I might need it tonight.

Nils left, but Lars stayed. He installed the parlor stove in the front room and built a fire. Then he sat in one of Mamma's good chairs and read Psalm 103 aloud, just like old times. I sat beside Papa and held his hand.

> *Bless the Lord, O my soul, and all that is within me,*
> *Bless His holy name. Bless the Lord, O my soul,*
> *And forget not all your benefits.*
> *Who forgives all your iniquities,*
> *Who heals all your diseases…*

The words softened my anger toward Lars. Papa's disease was not healed, but I had some benefits—a place to stay, a full stomach, friends who helped.

The phrase "who forgives all your iniquities" brought Adelle's words to my mind: *There's nothing grudging about God's forgiveness. He doesn't forgive part and harbor resentment over the rest. Forgive whole-heartedly, the way God forgives us.*

I let go of my anger. I felt relief. A calm peace began to fill my heart, and yet I was silent.

After reading, Lars disappeared into the loft. I heard him come down and pour hot water from the stove in the kitchen. Then I heard sounds like Papa's shaving. Lars appeared at the foot of Papa's bed, dressed in a brown wool suit. He moved his mouth as if to speak, but no sound came out. He didn't seem to know what to do with his hands. He cleared his throat, but he didn't speak.

"Is something the matter?" I asked.

"No, I—um," he stammered. He sucked in a breath, closing his eyes and standing taller, his shoulders broad and square. "*Ja.* Is somet'ing the matter."

I felt his eyes fully on me then.

"This morning… This morning you—you were angry with me. I felt your anger."

Silence. Long silence. Lars' eyes bored into mine.

So my manner had not been that of the gracious lady I wanted to be. Yet I did have cause for anger, didn't I? Had Lars meant to make me feel my anger was the problem, not his negligence? But I should not judge. I must admit my own faults.

I sighed and swallowed. "Yes. I was angry, angry and disappointed that no one told me about Papa earlier." I paused, trying to choose my words carefully.

"After all the time Papa and you and I spent together those months, I came to think of you as a friend. Even when I didn't hear from you, I thought of you as a friend. You were Papa's friend. I didn't blame you for taking Papa away from me. He made his own choice. But not letting me know he was so ill? That's not the kind of thing a friend does. What if my coming earlier would have saved him? What if the care I could have given him would have made a difference? I'd not be losing both my Papa and my Mamma."

A deep hurt crept into Lars's eyes. He looked away and then hung his head. The room was filled with a painful silence.

A sob stuck in my throat. *Stop, Annetti! You've only made things worse with your outburst. You torture the man's conscience! Remember what Adelle said. Vengeance is God's, not yours.*

He finally spoke. "I am here now. I am trying to be the friend I should have been."

Tears sprang to my eyes. I looked away.

"Please—don't turn away from me, Annetti. You have no idea how those wrongs have pained me. It is true that I never thought about your welfare. I was so happy that your father wanted to go with me and that he helped with building the church. I did not think what life would be like for you in Ashland without your father. He seemed to think that you'd be fine at your Tante Janna's and Onkel Peter's."

I looked at Papa as tears rolled down my cheeks. "Papa was mistaken." I held his hand to my cheek. "Papa, you have no idea how much I missed you. I didn't want to disappoint you, so I didn't write about my heartaches at Tante Janna's and Onkel Peter's. I had plenty." I said softly. "But I'm learning to let those go."

Papa grimaced, but he didn't open his eyes.

Lars continued. "And then last night Anna Skagerberg set me straight on several matters regarding you."

"She hardly knows me."

"She knows more than you think. She's as nosy as a bear in a honey pot, but she's also an astute judge of character. She seems to think you have more common sense than most women, that you are twice the woman that…" the words died on his lips.

My mind jumped to conclusions. *Twice the woman that Kelda is? Kelda, the blue-eyed beauty of your choice?* But I said nothing.

"Anna called me a fool for not snatching you up the first time we met."

I jerked my head up in surprise. "What? When you mistook me for a bear?"

His lips curled in a wistful smile. "*Nei*, I didn't tell Anna about that. I told her about that first dinner at your Tante Janna's house and all the vurk you did—oatmeal rolls, blackberry pie, washing dishes, and the meals I ate later with you and your Papa."

"*Ja*, vurk! Papa insisted on *vurk*," I sighed. It seemed I was only valued for my work. The thought discouraged me.

"The truth is I was too wrapped up in my own affairs at first to realize how serious your father's condition was. Even when I came to my senses, I didn't act. I respected your Papa's wishes. He didn't want you to worry. He expected to get better, and I trusted God to heal him. By the end, I knew I should have written to you about his illness weeks ago, but after—after—" He faltered again.

I looked up at him. I understood what he meant, and compassion for him filled my heart. "After Kelda broke your heart, you couldn't bring yourself to write to me?" I asked softly.

He nodded, keeping his eyes downcast, his thumbs fidgeting with the flaps of his jacket pockets. "I am sorry, Annetti. I am ashamed of myself. After everything between us, I lacked the courage. Please, please forgive the unkindness. I had no idea things would work out this way. I have agonized over why God would allow such a terrible thing, to lose both your mother and father."

How could I deny him this heartfelt request?

"I already have," I whispered. "As God has forgiven me, I forgive you."

"Thank you, oh, thank you, Annetti! I want to make things right. You do not have your father to take care of you now, but it is in my power to—" He faltered. "If you would consent—"

The words nearly died on his lips as he took in my startled gaze. He paused and inhaled deeply. "I want you to marry me, Annetti. I want to take care of you. I want to be a friend."

I stared at him, shocked. "This—this is hardly a good time to ask," I mumbled.

"No, it is the best time, under the circumstances. Your father can rest in peace if he knows I will take care of you." He looked down at Papa.

Papa had opened his eyes. Knowing eyes. He nodded his head ever so slightly.

"Oh, Papa!" I whispered. But he didn't answer. Before long, his eyes fluttered shut.

We sat in silence for a long while.

"Is that the only reason you ask me to marry you?" I finally replied. "To make things right between us?"

Silence. My heart cried out in anguish. *I don't want you to marry me out of pity and guilt, to assuage your conscience! You asked Kelda to marry you because you loved her. Why should I deserve less?* But I didn't speak.

Lars hesitated and then sighed. "I do not know. I am still trying to figure things out."

"Do you love me?" I asked, looking directly into his eyes. I watched them falter.

"Annetti, you are a good woman. I respect you. You're someone I could grow to love. Will you give me that chance?"

Though his words were honest, they cut my spirit to the quick. I wavered. I turned toward Papa.

He was watching. I forced a quivering smile. Papa's hand squeezed mine ever so slightly. "Say yes" his look seemed to plead.

How can I say "no" in Papa's presence?

The touch of Lars' hand on my shoulder startled me. I turned toward him.

"I could learn to love you, Annetti," he whispered. "Please."

"No. I won't marry you for the sake of your conscience." I hissed. I rubbed my temples and took a deep breath to calm myself. I forced my voice to sound even-tempered. "I will not agree to anything right now. I'm so tired I can hardly think straight."

Lars nodded numbly. He opened his mouth to speak, but nothing came out. Elon and Anna Skagerberg knocked at the shop door just then. They had come to check on Papa.

Mrs. Skagerberg had brought a loaf of bread and a jar of chicken broth. She tried dipping a piece of bread in the warm liquid and holding it to Papa's mouth. He sucked at the liquid but pushed the sop away with his tongue. She shook her head.

Before they left, Lars whispered something to Elon. A hushed conversation among the three followed. Then Anna turned and stared at me.

Her opinions were written all over her face, and I had no trouble reading them. I struggled to feel gracious toward her.

"Thank you for coming, Mr. and Mrs. Skagerberg. It was kind of you. But Papa is exhausted, and frankly, I am too."

Anna's eyes held mine. Then she nodded. "We'll be going. Are you sure you will be all right here alone?"

"Is there reason why I shouldn't be?"

Anna glanced at Elon and then shook her head. "When you want company, let me know."

Lars headed to the loft and came down with a bundle wrapped in a blanket, He left with the Skagerbergs.

I sat with Papa a while longer, but he never again stirred nor opened his eyes. Exhausted, I unpacked a flannel nightgown and slid the feather bolster out from under Papa's bed. I snuggled beneath two quilts, but sleep didn't come easily.

I slipped into a restless dream. I was at home in my own old room, lying in bed. Mamma was calling me to get up for breakfast: "Come, dear!" Then Papa called, "Karin!" Their voices sounded so close, so real that I blinked awake.

The fire in the stove had burned to a pile of black ash. The damp cold seeped through the covers. I sprang out of bed and turned up the wick of the flickering lamp. I blew gently on it until the flame burned more brightly. I looked at the clock. Three-thirty.

I touched Papa's cheek. Coldness seemed to flow from his flesh. I tucked my warm quilts around him. His mouth hung open. His face looked pale and gaunt. I rubbed his shoulders.

"I love you, Papa," I told him.

He was barely breathing.

I slid his hand from under the covers and lifted it to my cheek. "Oh God," I prayed aloud. "He trusted in you. Be near to us!"

Two gentle sighs escaped his lips, and then nothing.

"Papa!" I cried. I sat there weeping for the longest time, until I shivered with cold.

Despite the pain, I felt intensely grateful that God had allowed me to say good-bye to Papa, to witness his last moment on earth. My mamma had died while I slept. I only had Tante Janna's story of her last moments.

The cold stirred me to action. I built up the fire in both stoves, heated pots of water, and drank a cup of tea. I dressed myself in the old black muslin and started the laundry left from yesterday. I worked inside, by the lamplight. My tears dripped into the washtub, but I scrubbed on through sheer force of will. Papa and his "vurk" stayed on my mind. There was nowhere to hang the laundry, as the items from the previous day had not yet fully dried. I left the wet clothes in two galvanized washtubs.

Then I forced myself to change the soiled linens and to wash my father's body. Papa had washed Mamma, though at the time I had never understood how he had borne the task. Now I understood. It was the last act of love. I was no longer a child.

I covered his body with a quilt. I ended up ironing his clothes dry and hanging them before the stove to finish even though the dampness wouldn't have mattered. The cold couldn't bother him now.

I worked through a blur of emotions. Work was how Papa had coped. It was how I would survive now—how I must survive.

19: The End and the Beginning

By six o'clock in the morning, I had finished everything and sponged myself clean. I dressed in the plum-colored suit Papa had cajoled me to make for myself. I pinned up my hair and tied a sheer black veil over the plum-colored hat.

I shuddered, thinking of a long, lonely day by myself. I couldn't stand that. Not today. Not with Papa lying dead in the front room. Hunger gnawed at my ribs. Every muscle drooped with weariness, but there were things to be done today. I had to arrange for Papa's burial.

Anna Skagerberg served a hearty breakfast—solid enough to last the mill men and lumberjacks to dinnertime. I figured it would do for me as well. The meal had already started when I slipped quietly in, savoring the heady aroma from the kitchen. Katrina was pouring coffee. Nils sat at the end of a table, Elmer in one arm and Dieter on his knee. The men were teasing him about holding the baby. He bore their taunts with a grin.

"*Ja*, and would you like *me* to pour your coffee instead?" he joked back. "Do you think it would end up in your cup?"

The men guffawed at that remark. Katrina looked at him reproachfully, and the men laughed at her reaction.

"I tell you, Katrina. They are just jealous of my beautiful wife and my two fine boys. What a treasure!" He looked from Katrina to Dieter affectionately. "I have heard rumors that someone here intends—" His eyes flitted merrily from face to face, but he stopped mid-sentence when they fell suddenly on mine. The grin that had creased his face flattened.

The men hushed, surprised, and followed his eyes to where I stood. I nodded a brisk hello. One of the men started to elbow Lars, but I averted my eyes.

So the news of Lars' intentions was common knowledge now—thanks, undoubtedly, to Anna's indomitable gossip. Yet here I was, driven to count on her kindness for breakfast.

Well, no time like the present to grow tough and strong!

I turned and bounded up the steps to the half-landing and descended into the kitchen. Anna didn't notice me at first.

I stood quietly relishing the noise. To be with people, with the living—that was what my soul craved now. I listened to the sounds of life—the murmur of table talk, the clink of silverware on dishes, sausages sizzling in the pan, and Anna's absent-minded clucking to herself.

She turned. My quiet pose startled her, but Anna Skagerberg was sharp. She knew in an instant that Papa had died, and any disapproval from the evening before vanished. She hovered about me, murmuring "poor dear" and patting my shoulder.

"I came for breakfast," I said numbly.

"Of course, dear," she responded. "Here, sit at this little table beside the window. I will fix you a plate." Miraculously, a plate full of pancakes, eggs, and sausage appeared before me. Then she left me to myself and returned to the stove. I ate ravenously.

I heard Elmer fussing. The buzz of conversation in the dining room shifted. Katrina brought Elmer to the kitchen to rock while Mrs. Skagerberg replenished the serving bowls and platter.

"Never mind the men, Annetti," Katrina advised. She smiled. "They're wild, but they don't mean any harm. Not these men. Anna won't tolerate a good-for-nothing among her boarders."

I took another bite but didn't say a word.

"You look very nice today, but I can tell that you're already worn out. Were you up all night? How is your Papa?"

I swallowed. "The strangest thing happened," I said, glad for her company. I told her about the dream. Tears streamed down my face as I spoke of Papa's death, but my voice remained calm. "I have to figure out what to do now."

"You can't stay there, Annetti," Katrina announced.

I hadn't expected such a response. "And why not?"

"You're only seventeen, and you have no one to protect you. You don't know this town. News spreads fast. If drunks found out you were living alone, there'd be no end to the constant harassment. Besides, your mamma would turn over in her grave if she knew. *My* mamma would take a train here to escort you back home. You don't want that. It is not a good idea to live alone."

I had not anticipated the possibility of danger. In Ashland, I had always moved in the safe circles of church and family. I had never really been alone. I hadn't thought of the protection marriage offered a single woman.

"But what can I do?" I asked reluctantly.

"Stay with us, Annetti. Move your things into one of the spare bedrooms. Perhaps you can work for Anna. She doesn't pay much, but you'd have your food and enough to rent a room. I've been helping her out in a pinch, but I'm not worth much now with both Elmer and Dieter to look after. Winter will be here soon, and I don't want to take Elmer out every day in the inclement weather."

With my mouth puckered and twisted to one side, I paused to consider this option. In ways, I resented the suggestion. Was the danger that great? Papa had paid for the house. It would be mine. It *should* be mine. Why leave it and pay rent, to become a servant all over again? If I stayed with Katrina's family, I'd be expected to help with housework. I might not ever be able to open the shop.

I felt trapped. I knew that I could never refuse requests such as "Annetti, would you keep an eye on Dieter while I..." or "Annetti, the water pail is empty. Could you refill it on your way back from the outhouse?" I wouldn't begrudge a reasonable amount of help, of course, but I knew firsthand how expectations grow. I sighed.

"Thank you so much for the offer, Katrina. I need a bit of time to think about it. Could I get back with you later today? I truly appreciate your advice as well as the offer."

Nils appeared and kissed Katrina before leaving for work. I heard the sound of the men shuffling out the front door, still joshing with each other.

Katrina rose and asked, "Here, would you mind holding Elmer? I need to help Anna with the dishes." She deposited him in my arms before I had time to consent.

See what I mean? I said to myself. There I sat, at the little table beneath the window, my back to the stairs, holding a newborn babe on the day of my father's demise. *Life and death,* I thought. *Two extremes in one day...and that dream of Mamma and Papa! What a strange day! But I had wanted to be with the living...*

I heard movement behind me then. Lars stood on the steps. I wondered how long he had been there and whether he planned to stay at Anna's boardinghouse now.

"Your Papa passed?" he asked.

I nodded. "This morning. Early."

"I am sorry—but I thank God that you were able to see him!" He moved to sit in the chair opposite me "What will you do next?"

I shrugged.

"You will need a coffin and a burial plot. As your Papa's friend, I would like to make the coffin. Our church has a small plot on the side. No one has been buried there yet, but you are welcome to bury your Papa there."

"Thank you, Lars," I responded softly.

"Do you want some kind of ceremony?"

We'd had a funeral service for Mamma. Pastor Lyndahl had spoken. But now? The answer came to me, unbidden. "I would like you to speak, Lars. You were Papa's best friend."

I looked up into his eyes. They were filled with tears. He nodded and left without a word. My heart sank. *With this help, he will have done his duty by my father. He won't ask again what he asked last night. No one truly wants a marriage based purely on duty. Surely he didn't either. But if he had loved me, truly loved me, he would not have given up so easily.* Oh, the conflicting emotions!

I had traveled to Cloquet on Wednesday. Papa died early Friday morning. That morning, I spoke with Anna Skagerberg about working for her until I could open up the shop. I had to listen to her thoughts on several subjects before she settled down to agree that, yes, she did want my help and I could start on Monday. I endured patiently, biting my bottom lip as she scolded.

"Annetti! How could you break the heart of that dear boy? Hasn't his heart been broken enough? And to snub the kindness of such a godly man! Don't you realize how much courage it took for him to face you? And to offer marriage? He was trying to do something noble and kind, and you made him feel inadequate and ashamed. I thought you had more sense!"

I looked down and paused before I answered her. "I am sorry, Anna, but I do not wish to discuss that subject with you," I told her as firmly as I could without being rude.

Her accusation jarred me. *Had I broken Lars's heart?* I had privately accused Kelda of that very thing. And yet I wondered.

How could I have broken his heart, if I hadn't in some way won it first? Was there hope? Or had Anna confused his heart with his conscience?

I ended up spending most of the day by myself after all. I scrubbed the shop from loft to cellar and piled the clean bedding on the kitchen table. My hands were chapped after all the laundry and scrubbing. I felt relieved to move on to the ironing, which I decided to haul to Katrina's kitchen. I couldn't stand any more solitude. Some of ironing I recognized as Papa's. Some must have belonged to Lars, but I ironed it anyway.

Lars did not say a word to me after Friday breakfast. He avoided me at meals, which I ate by myself in Anna's kitchen. *Was his heart broken, as Anna said? Had he given up on me?* My thoughts pained me. *Work! I need to work and not feel!*

Friday evening, Nils helped me move my bed and mattress to their spare room. I had no desire to sleep in the shop with Papa's body lying in full view. It seemed my future was laid out for me. I felt a dull resignation.

Before supper on Saturday evening, Lars broke his silence. "We have a burial to take care of before we eat," he told the crowd of Anna's boarders. Follow, if you wish." He glanced at me.

I followed the men to the shop. They lifted Papa's body into the casket Lars had made and carried it to the churchyard. Lars spoke briefly of Papa's friendship and his eternal hope. I cast my handful of dirt. Nils and some of the boarders hurriedly covered the grave. I could tell they were eager to be done with the chilly task. They wanted to eat, to enjoy a meal.

I stood alone and watched. Katrina had not come to the service. She and her children were already at Anna's house. When the men finished, I turned toward the Skagerberg's home.

Lars hurried after me, brushing his gloved hand across my back. "Annetti, I would like a word with you, please."

I stopped in my tracks. "Here?"

"Yes. I want you to know—it wasn't right of me to expect you to make a decision so quickly, under pressure. I still want you to be my wife. I do. However long it takes for you to decide, Annetti, I will wait for you."

I bent my head down, hoping that the glimmer of light from the houses on Avenue G would not shine on the tears streaming from my eyes. But my tears dropped, catching the gleam anyway. *Please let me be wrong,* I silently prayed. *Dear God! Let him love me.*

"You are crying!" he exclaimed, gathering me in his arms.

I let my head rest against his shoulder. How long had it been since someone had embraced me so kindly? Such care was a luxury. *Perhaps, perhaps—*

"It is cold," he stated. "We should go inside."

He caught my elbow and escorted me to the Skagerberg's back porch, where the yellow light from the kitchen streamed across the steps. The men were forbidden to enter this way, invading Anna's culinary domain. Nevertheless, Lars drew me inside before the stove, pulling off my gloves and warming my chapped hands with his own.

Amazingly, the kitchen was empty. I could hear Anna's voice rising above the voices of the men as she ladled out soup in the front room, but it was Lars' voice that captivated my heart.

"Annetti, when I left Thursday evening, I took with me the letters you'd written to your Papa. Perhaps I shouldn't have done so, as they belonged to your Papa, not to me. But I took them because at the time, as awkward as things were between us, they seemed the only way I might get to know you better."

I stared up at him, surprised. *Those were my letters on the chest? Not Kelda's?*

"Your Papa saved all of your letters, you know. I'd often see him reading and re-reading them. Sometimes he'd read parts aloud to me because he enjoyed them so much. You must know how much he loved you, Annetti. And he loved the Lord. He's in heaven with God now, a better place by far."

"Yes," I said softly, wiping my tears.

"So I read your letters and re-read them over the past few days. They reminded me what I'd forgotten—those evenings we used to spend reading the Scriptures together."

"Your letters were full of substance. You read the Scriptures on your own, and you thought about them deeply. You didn't write about your troubles, but knowing now that you struggled with troubles during that time, I began to understand how God was shaping your thoughts, bringing His steady and loving and cheerful nature to light in your life."

His words were like yeast to bread dough. They made my spirit rise.

"Annetti, your question the other night shook me. Do I love you? I am embarrassed to admit I'd only been thinking of duty. You made me reconsider the basis of the marriage I proposed. I found I'd forgotten the one great commandment to husbands in Ephesians chapter five: Husbands, love your wives. And so what you asked of me—do I love you?—was an honest and reasonable expectation."

I looked down. "You told me you were still trying to figure things out."

"And I have, Annetti. These last few days I have watched your quiet courage, your kindness, and your tender love of Dieter and little Elmer. I loved your father for those same traits. It is only natural to love you, Annetti."

My tears flowed freely again. I didn't try to stop them. *Thank God he didn't mention work!*

Lars cupped my face in his hands. "I don't know when I started truly loving you, Annetti, whether it was the letters that drew me or the memory of those happy months I ate meals with you and your Papa. But I know this now: I love you with all my heart. I choose to love you, and I promise I always will. I will be here to take care of you, if God allows me—if you allow me."

I saw that love flowing from his eyes, and pure joy sprang from my heart. "I love you too," I whispered. "I have for a long, long time."

Lars' face burst into broad and happy grin. "It feels good to be loved, *ja?*"

I nodded and rested my head on his shoulder. He stroked my hair with his hand.

"Annetti, I have something for you," he said softly. "I hope it is something that you will agree to keep." From his coat pocket he produced a small velvet bag.

I looked at him, my eyes wide with questions. From the bag he slipped a narrow gold band set with a smoky amethyst. I drew in my breath sharply, noticing the color, rejoicing in the color. *The stone matched my eyes, not Kelda's!*

"For you, Annetti. Will you be my wife?"

I threw my arms about him.

Someone walked through the door. I heard the steps and the flap of the swinging door, though my face was turned away, buried in Lars' embrace. The footsteps stopped abruptly. Then they hurried away, leaving the door to jaw back and forth.

Soon we heard the buzz of hushed conversations, then the clinking of spoons against tin cups. "Hear ye! Hear ye! The preacher has an announcement," someone declared loudly. There were guffaws in the background.

Lars held me at arms' length and looked directly into my eyes. "That is yes, I think? You must be sure, Annetti. You are ready for a big fuss?"

I nodded and gave him a shy smile.

Lars grasped my hand and pulled me through the kitchen door, grinning with pleasure. He raised his free hand to hush the crowd, but the men only grew wilder.

"Hey, fellas!" someone yelled. "She's blushing. Lars must have kissed her."

"Hah! Kissing in the kitchen. Now the preacher boy is going to have to tie the knot! And we all thought he was hopeless!"

"Sweet potatoes! You work fast," another voice interjected. "I didn't know you had it in you. She only arrived a few days ago!" Guffaws rose.

"Lars, you old coot! You're a sly one."

"And I was going to ask her out to dinner," another voice whined.

More guffaws followed. "Didn't even give us a chance!"

The men teased Lars as one of their own, while I stood with his arm around me. Strangely, I didn't mind the teasing. Katrina was right. The men were wild, but good-natured. It seemed the happiest teasing of my life.

How strange people are, I thought. *These men have just helped me bury my father, and here they are, as jolly as can be, eager to embrace life.*

I ignored the winks and grins until one of the men exclaimed, "Oh, by gosh, it's true! She has a ring!"

I held it up for all to see. Papa had just died, but I was grinning and laughing. It felt strangely good to be happy and alive.

"Of course, it's true," Lars said with a laugh. "Did you think I would kiss her without giving her a ring first?"

Then all of them—Nils included—clinked their forks against their cups, demanding he kiss me, then and there. I blushed as Lars caught me in his arms. He kissed me long and fierce until my body relaxed and melted into his. The men clapped and cheered.

Another ordeal awaited me the following morning at church. I had intended to sit quietly at the back of the chapel and observe, unnoticed. However, news of our engagement rippled through the congregation. People would sit down and exchange a few quiet words; then they would turn and look toward me. Many rose to greet me and introduce themselves.

Katrina sat with me and was kind enough to repeat their names and fill in details whenever a brief lull provided a moment of respite. I was overwhelmed with unanswerable questions and unsolicited comments.

"When is the wedding? We'd love to be invited."

"Finally! That young man needs a good wife to look after him. He's much too thin and rumpled."

"You must both come by for dinner this week. How about Thursday? Six o'clock?"

"Do you need anything, dearie? We'll be glad to help."

"Oh, Merton, she looks so young. Do you remember those fond days? How old are you, darling? Only seventeen? Not much older than I was!"

Lars had secluded himself in the tiny office to the left of the altar. He needed time to prepare and pray before his sermon, he had told me. So, I made up answers without his help, inwardly laughing at my sudden popularity. I vowed to enjoy these dear people, the "flock" of my preacher-husband-to-be. I wanted know them and love them too.

Lars preached about Abraham's servant and the choosing of a wife for Abraham's son. He explained God's leading in the arranged marriage between Isaac and Rebekah. He focused on Isaac's meditation, Rebekah's willingness, and God's preparation of their hearts.

The story made everyone's mouths twitch with smiles. I nearly cried at the end, at the part about Isaac loving Rebekah and thus being comforted in the death of his mother. Sweet Lars in his kindness was doing the same for me at the death of Papa. He never said so much in words, but I felt his comfort.

After the service, Elsa Skelton made a point of seeking me out. "We live right behind your Papa's shop, Annetti. Andrew was a good man. Lars is too. You can be proud of them both. When you get settled, come over some time for a cup of tea."

Annetti

We ate at Anna Skagerberg's after church, and Lars decided that we may as well be married quietly the next day, as neither of us could afford a big wedding. The following morning, he walked me to the office of the Justice of the Peace, where we purchased a marriage license and spoke our vows. It all seemed so business-like. I didn't feel married.

I helped Anna in the kitchen the rest of the day. Lars had a quiet talk with her after supper, and she sent us home with food for the next day. Afterward, he walked me to Katrina's house and hauled my things back to the shop. The day was full of errands.

Lars took apart Papa's bedstead. I helped him move it to the loft. While he assembled it there, I busied myself with straightening up the rooms and putting away the laundry. In doing so, I discovered the bundle of letters tied in a pink ribbon.

They were my letters to Papa—the ones Lars had read and treasured. I found no trace of Kelda's correspondence anywhere in the house. I smiled with pleasure. My husband may have been slow to love me, but his heart was honest and true.

The evening wore on. I decided to use the outhouse before retiring, not wishing to face the lack of privacy accompanied by chamber pots. I hadn't taken a candle to light my way. As I picked my way through the back yard lit by the moon, a dark figure startled me as I stumbled into the doorway of the outhouse. I gasped.

"Annetti!" Lars exclaimed. He caught me in a full embrace, pulling me against himself and kissing me soundly. "I've wanted to do that all day, Annetti, my dear wife."

"Oh, don't, please!"

"What—kiss you? Or call you my dear wife?"

"Don't squeeze me like that when I need to use the outhouse," I responded, stepping around him to reach the stall and relieve my need. "You can kiss me all you want otherwise—after I've washed my hands," I called from inside the stall.

Lars laughed that full, ringing laugh I remembered so fondly. I suddenly realized how sorely I had missed it.

"A wife is a good thing! Your Papa used to tell me that frequently."

"I told you once before that scheming fathers were far more dangerous than scheming mothers," I said.

Lars laughed. "In this case, I don't mind. I think that I am going to like you as my wife. In fact, I know I am!" He waited until I had finished and washed my hands, and then he kissed me again until I shivered with cold. "You go inside. Warm up. I will bring in the wood and draw water."

I followed his directions, but inwardly I churned. I feared this night in ways. Neither Papa nor Mamma had ever told me what happens between a man and his wife. I had overheard the giggled whispers of Kelda's friends after her wedding. I'd seen the affection that Nils showed Katrina, and I surmised that what they shared must have been both enjoyable and pleasant.

Nevertheless, the unknown scared me. I knitted in the front room while Lars undressed and washed. I was glad when he retired to the loft, leaving a fresh tub of water for me before the warmth of the stove in the kitchen. He had even thought to hang blankets over the windows.

I took my time bathing—soaking in the steaming, fragrant liquid. I had doused the bathwater with one of Mamma's packets of herbs, and the relaxing aroma wafted pleasantly about me. I unbraided and combed my hair. It fell in waves about my back. I rubbed down with a towel and slipped on the silk nightgown I had made for Kelda's wedding. I had just dimmed the lantern when I heard a sigh from above.

"Annetti, you are so beautiful!"

Startled, I looked up and flushed with color. Lars lay on his stomach, with his arms folded at the edge of the loft. He rested his chin on his crossed wrists. He grinned with pleasure.

"You were watching me!" I accused.

He laughed aloud. "*Ja*, I am your husband now, remember? It is my job now to look after you. I was looking."

I threw my hairbrush at him and glared, but he only caught it and laughed again. "Those lavender eyes! How could I ever forget them! Come and keep your promise about those kisses."

I blushed again as I climbed the ladder to the loft. He read to me from the Song of Solomon, and we prayed and dedicated our marriage to the honor of our Savior.

Then we sang a Scandinavian wedding hymn, Lars's tenor voice intertwining with the melody of my soprano. We sang with pure devotion. Then he kissed me and tenderly taught me what I did not know about marriage.

20: The Blackberry Jam Fairy Tale

Morning brought new sensations of joy. Lying on my side, I awoke to the stroke of Lars' hand along the curve of my waist and hip. Yawning, I sat up. I swung my feet to the cold floor and stretched. The sun shone bright through the dormer behind me. I turned to look. A layer of ice covered the world outside. The sun glinted off the shimmering branches.

"Your work!" I exclaimed to Lars, realizing how late it must be. I jumped up and looked out the window, trying to guess the time from the amount of light.

"I have already told the builder I would not come today."

I looked down at him, questioning.

He grinned at me. "Honeymoon. I stay with you all day today and tomorrow."

"I don't know anything about honeymoons," I admitted shyly.

"There is time to learn," he promised, a playful smile tugging at his lips. He reached to pull me back into bed, but I pulled away with a grin of my own.

"If it starts with a kiss and hug, you'll have to race me to the outhouse," I replied. I dashed to the ladder and scrambled down, grabbing his coat from the kitchen chair and slipping on the large boots that sat on the back porch.

"Thief!" he called out after me. He had pulled on his long underwear and stood in the doorway watching. "Please do not fall!"

So he had to wait, and while he took his turn and drew water and hauled in more wood, I built up the fire and brushed and braided my hair. It didn't stay bound for long.

By the next day, we had begun to settle into a comfortable routine of amiable teasing. I felt very much at home and very married. I could smile with ease at the naiveté of my first uneasy evening. Often I thought of Papa and wondered if he could see me from heaven. I reveled in the comfort that Lars brought to my soul. Did Papa know how much joy we had found together?

The elation was mutual. "Living with you is so much better than living alone," Lars commented on Thursday morning.

He hugged me from behind as I sliced bread for breakfast.

"Do you think it wise to startle me when I have a knife in my hands?" I calmly asked, shaking off the caresses that ensued.

"I trust you with my life," Lars joked.

I tried another tack. "I like my bread sliced evenly. You make concentrating very difficult, you know."

He just laughed and kissed me. "My Annetti!"

"How did you ever manage without me?" I inquired.

"I vurked," he replied, his words and his accent reminding me of Papa's. "I did not realize what I was missing. I knew you were a good woman, Annetti, but I never suspected life would be so good like this! God has given us more than I ever dreamed."

"Hmmm," I replied, marveling at my own change of thought.

It no longer mattered to me what he had written to Kelda months ago. Lars loved *me* with the wild and reckless love of discovery. He loved me as if I were a treasure-box of gems from which he could neither withdraw his gaze nor detach his heart.

I watched the glint of the amethyst ring as I finished slicing, treasuring his thoughtfulness. He may not have anticipated the strength of my love or its deep passion, but he remembered the lavender. I couldn't have been more pleased.

This morning I drew out the jars of jam that had lain at the bottom of Mamma's trunk. Oh, such memories! They sparked a mischievous plan in my mind. I finished slicing the bread and plopped the jars on the table with a flourish.

"Once upon a time," I announced as we sat to eat, "a handsome young preacher expressed a wish for jam made by a certain maiden with lavender eyes."

"Was it strawberry or blackberry?" Lars asked with a grin.

"Both," I replied. "He was hungry. He liked to eat."

"Well, that part's true," Lars responded.

"Ah! But he was a clever fiend!" I continued. "He tried to trick the maiden into thinking that she had promised to make him jam, but she saw through his plot. Yet she thought of the young man day and night. Then one day, he left. Soon afterward, she relented. She picked berries and made jam."

"She stashed the jars among her treasures, waiting for the day when he would remember. You see, she had grown to love him, thinking of him so often—"

I faltered, my eyes filling with tears as I gazed at Lars. *He is so dear to me!* I hadn't expected this sudden emotion.

Astonishment flashed across his face. "I—I am sorry, Annetti. I never knew you loved me then."

"And I never told you. I didn't dare to admit it, fearing it could never be true, especially when—" I halted. I hadn't meant to dredge up pain.

Realization and then guilt crossed his face. "It must have been awful for you, Annetti."

I nodded, teary-eyed. "More than you know. I ached with every letter K—"

"Please, do not even say her name. I was a fool, such a fool."

"But now you're wise," I countered, trying to brighten his spirit. "It's better this way. You found out what you needed to learn on your own, and that adventure makes ours so much more joyful."

A tender smile spread across Lars' face. "Cheerful and steady and loving—I love that about you, Annetti. You draw from a deep well of wisdom. Anna Skagerberg told me Monday evening that I had chosen better than I knew. I am inclined to believe her."

I smiled at him fondly, "I like her wording. Mmmm. Chosen. Chosen by you."

"That's so!" He leaned over and kissed me.

I sighed. "I'm just glad that the story has a happy ending. The maiden found her true love. The handsome young preacher married her and gave her an amethyst ring and"—I added with a playful glint in my eye—"loved her as often as she liked."

Lars' eyebrow rose with a curious twitch. "But today the young preacher must go to vurk."

"Oh, pity!" I quipped merrily, spreading jam on my bread. "I don't think his mind will be on his work at all." My eyes flashed with laughter. "I hope that he can do his work as well as he attends to his marital duties." I smirked at Lars, and he grinned.

Afterward, we headed off to work—Lars toward the builder and I toward Anna Skagerberg's boarding house.

Later that evening, I eyed the crates from Adelle that still sat under the counter, unopened. "Your mother sent you those crates, you know. You haven't opened them yet."

Lars looked puzzled. "She did?"

"Yes! I guess I forgot to tell you earlier. The Sunday before I left, she cornered me at church and told me that she had a gift for you. She asked me if I could make sure that it was delivered. I don't know how she knew that I was leaving on Wednesday—" I faltered, aware of a blush on Lars' cheeks.

"What was it that you told me one day? About scheming mothers?" he asked.

I raised an eyebrow. "You forget. It was scheming fathers who concerned me, not scheming mothers. Oh, my goodness! You don't mean your mother—"

"I'm afraid so."

"Huh! Why don't we just look and find out?"

The first few crates held treasures for our new home: a supply of homemade candles, a framed cross-stitched rendering of Psalm 23, a beautiful crocheted bedspread that must have taken Adelle hours to complete, monogrammed dishtowels and handkerchiefs.

From the others, we unloaded staples—a sack of flour, cheese wheels, dried blueberries and apples, a crock of butter, a jar of honey, and seasonings of every sort. My favorite was the array of seeds from Adelle's garden, a whole set of herbs and vegetables and flowers along with detailed instructions.

"She knew somehow that we'd end up marrying," I marveled. I felt a gush of affection for Adelle. *She trusted God. She knew my heart. She knew I would forgive.*

"We'll have to write your mother and tell her the good news—and thank her, of course. Goodness! Where did I put my stationery? I'll write to her now."

"Can that wait, Annetti? I had other plans in mind for the evening," Lars said, glancing longingly up toward the loft.

It was my turn to grin. "Well then, sure. First things first!"

So our marriage began. The years were as sweet as blackberry jam.

*After her husband's fatal accident,
Cherry Hanson finds a box of pickings
in the remains of his car. Among the antique
kitchen utensils, she discovers a tin tole box
filled with letters a century old.*

*As Cherry struggles to put her life back together,
Annetti's letters to her friend Elsa puzzle and
intrigue her. How did letters from Minnesota end
up in South Carolina? What happened to the
families of the two women?*

*Cherry sets out to find answers
and in the process finds far more
than she ever expected.*

Sequel to ANNETTI Coming Soon!

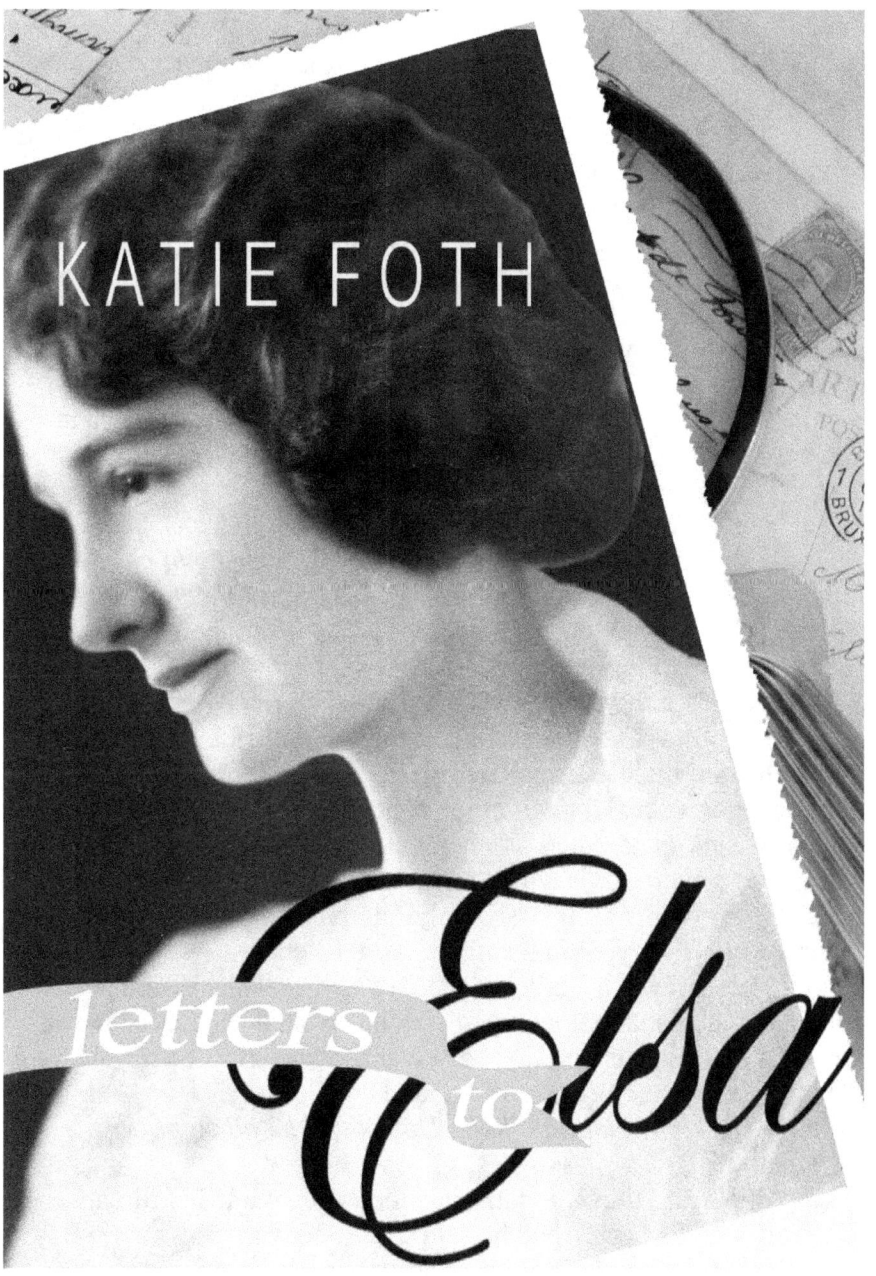

LETTERS TO ELSA
1: The Tin Tole Box

"Of course he would!" Cherry Hanson muttered to herself as she pulled a crate from the back seat of the '66 Chrysler.

The old piece of junk was no great loss to her. She had hated driving it. The trunk had been rusted out ages ago. The vinyl seats were cracked and split open. The glove compartment perpetually hung agape. Why, the car had to be coddled and jury-rigged, or it balked when it started—if it started.

Haywood Hanson had been the only one with enough patience to fiddle with the cursed car. If only Hay had sold it to the junk dealer last week! But no, Hay decided he could sweet-talk a few more weeks out of his Maizy. The old girl had stalled on a turn and betrayed him. Left him stranded in the intersection for some careless kid to careen into.

Oh, Hay! Why couldn't you die at home, like a normal person? But no, you had to drive an hour to Abbeville to meet your fate. You were picking again, weren't you? Even though you knew we don't have money for such hobbies. That strike-it-rich dream of yours left your children with no father, your wife with no husband.

Tears sprang to her eyes. Hay had died on Tuesday exactly one week before. The funeral had been held on Friday, attended by tons of his old buddies from Clemson University, but no relatives on his side. His dad had died of colon cancer when Hay was in middle school. His mom had died of a heart attack two years after Cherry and Hay had married. Hay had been the only child of parents who were also without siblings. The only relatives who had come to the funeral were Cherry's mom and her Aunt Ellen.

The garage had called yesterday asking if she would please collect any personal belongings from the crashed car. Tuesday was always a slow day at The Coffee Whisk, so she'd closed the shop for the afternoon to take care of the errand.

"Hush now, Cherry, love. Things will be all right. Just you wait and see."

She heard the words in her mind. They made her throat ache with sorrow. How often had he said that? She was the worrier. Hay was the rock. His optimism never failed him. If only he were still here now to hold her and encourage her and work his marvelous charms! He always had some trick up his sleeve to make ends meet, the friend of a friend of a friend who needed a hand with something. But now his sleeve and helping hands were buried in the graveyard, along with every last cent from their savings account.

"Would you like help with that, ma'am?" The gentle timbre of the man's voice lent her comfort. Kind eyes pleaded with her from a face the color of latte.

"Thank you, but I can manage. Thanks for calling me." Cherry lifted the crate from the trunk and packed it into the back of her '93 Nissan Quest. She nudged the trunk door to make sure it latched properly. If it didn't, the inside lights would stay on and drain the battery overnight. Another worry settled over her. *How long will the old van last? Hay always kept it tuned up for me. If it gives out, how will I manage?*

She picked up the kids from Pendleton Elementary on her way home. As usual, Logan sat sullen in the front bucket seat, staring out the side window.

I wish I knew what he was thinking. He shrugs off my every attempt to talk. Is that just a phase fifth-grade boys go through, or is it because his father's death hit him so hard? Hay would have known how to cajole a few sentences out of him, how to make him laugh...

Madison chattered from the middle bench seat all the way home. Cherry glanced at her the rear view mirror. Her third-grader's bright blue eyes danced, and her platinum blond ponytail bobbed with every move of her expressive face. Madison looked like Cherry with her slender build and fair complexion, but she possessed Hay's sunny disposition and outgoing personality.

"Miss Kavetta is the best, Mom. She's collecting milk cartons. When the class has enough, Miss Kavetta will invite us to an after-school party. We're going to build an igloo and have dog-sled races and roast fish over an open fire. You'll let me go, won't you?"

"Of course, honey."

"Only buy the clear plastic milk jugs, Mom," Madison begged. "Miss Kavetta said they let the light inside better. She doesn't want the solid white or yellow plastic ones. They're supposed to look like blocks of ice."

"Will do, but you know we're not racing through more milk than usual just for your social studies unit on Eskimos. We have to watch our pennies now that Dad's gone."

"We've always watched our pennies, even when Dad was here." Logan's tone sounded sour and flat.

"Well, we have to watch them even more closely now. Was there something you wanted, Logan?" Cherry asked, as she turned the van into the steep driveway of their little house on Grand Oak Circle. "Is your class working on a project too? You know I'll find a way to help if I possibly can."

No answer. Logan was still staring out the side window. The back of his golden head was hard to read. The boy looked like Hay—tall and muscular, with a rugged handsomeness that turned heads his direction.

Cherry sighed. *He's an introvert and a worrier just like me. You'd think that would make things easier for me to connect with him. Not! Guess I'll need to e-mail Mr. Berry to find out what's up with his class.*

"I made molasses cookies this morning. Help yourself to a snack before you go out to play," Cherry said as they pulled into the garage. "And don't leave your stuff in the van. Hang your backpacks on the hooks by the door."

She unloaded the crate of odds and ends and set it on a stack of boxes against the wall. *More stuff to go through.* She rummaged through the crate.

Looks like someone was cleaning out the kitchen drawers in an old house. Old-fashioned kitchen utensils. I can add those to the wall of The Coffee Whisk. Maybe I'll sell a few. A box of kitchen matches. Useless. A stack of old aprons. Maybe I can sell some of these to Mountain Made. They seem to be well-preserved.

Cherry picked up a yellowed cookbook. A string through its punched holes held the pages together. "Our Savior's Lutheran Church, Cloquet, Minnesota," the title read.

Interesting! How did that end up here, in South Carolina? Might want to browse through the recipes...

Buried at the bottom was a vintage tole tin box covered with flowers.

Now this might be worth something! Blue Ridge Antiques might snap it up.

Cherry opened the box. Inside lay two bundles of small envelopes, tied with a ribbon. She picked them up and read the neat slanted script.

Curious! They're addressed to Elsa Skelton in Duluth, Minnesota. Postmarked in Cloquet, Minnesota. Sent by someone named Annetti Sorenson.

She glanced at the postmark.

No way! May 1902? The letters have probably sat inside this tin for over a hundred years. This might be worth something! Where did Hay find this? Likely in one of Abbeville's grand old homes where he loved picking. But which one?

The February cold sent a chill up Cherry's spine. Or was it the thrill Hay always sought when he was picking? Either way, she needed a cup of coffee. Cherry took the cookbook and the tin box inside. *Drat!* Logan had left the milk jug out again.

"Logan?"

No answer. She looked down the hall. His door was shut. Probably on his computer, the old one Hay had let Logan take when they'd bought the kitchen iPad.

"Mom, can I watch?" Madison asked.

Cherry grimaced. "I hate to let you start this early. It seems the TV stays on all evening once you start. What did you want to watch?"

"Miss Kavetta said she'd give us extra credit for each episode of the *Mercy Street* series we watched. We just have to write a paragraph about what we liked best.

"That would be OK, I guess. Just turn it off afterward, please."

Cherry fixed herself a latte and settled on a stool at the kitchen island. She slipped the top envelope from the stack of letters and opened the crinkly paper carefully. The first page was written on old-fashioned onionskin. The following pages looked as if they'd been ripped out of a diary. She sipped her coffee as she read.